A Life Not Chosen

The story of Ethlyn Trapp
and her father

A prominent daughter of a British Columbian pioneer
and New Westminster elder statesman

STEWART JACKSON

A Life Not Chosen

National Library of Canada Cataloguing in Publication Data
Jackson, Stewart M.
    A life not chosen
The story of Ethlyn Trapp, OC, and her father
    Includes biographical notes and bibliography.
    ISBN: 978-1-4251-8459-9 (soft cover)
1. 1. History—British Columbia—New Westminster—
The BC Cancer Institute—Klee Wyck

Stewart M Jackson
North Vancouver, BC
sandjjackson@shaw.ca

A life not chosen
The story of Ethlyn Trapp, OC, and her father
Stewart Jackson

Design by Ernest Stelzer

Jacket photographs of Ethlyn Trapp and her father,
Thomas John Trapp
Background: *Cabin in the Woods*, Emily Carr.

Note for Librarians: A cataloguing record for this book is available from Library
and Archives Canada at www.collectionscanada.ca/amicus/index-e.html

Printed in Victoria, BC, Canada.

ISBN: 978-1-4251-8459-9 (soft cover)

*Our mission is to efficiently provide the world's finest, most comprehensive
book publishing service, enabling every author to experience success.
To find out how to publish your book, your way, and have it available
worldwide, visit us online at www.trafford.com*

Trafford rev. 8/25/2009

Order this book online at www.trafford.com
or email orders@trafford.com

Most Trafford titles are also available at major online book retailers.

 www.trafford.com

North America & international
toll-free: 1 888 232 4444 (USA & Canada)
phone: 250 383 6864 ♦ fax: 812 355 4082

Contents

Acknowledgements

Throughout the research for this book I have greatly appreciated the help and professionalism of staff members from several archives, libraries and museums. I would particularly like to thank Jack Ziebart of the Vancouver Island Military Museum; Wendy Hunt of the BCMA Archives; Danielle Currie and Peter Johnson of the Vancouver Art Gallery; Robert Turner, curator emeritus of the Royal BC Museum and Archives; Judy Root of the British Columbia Archives; staff of the New Westminster Archives and the Vancouver City Archives; Diana Hall of the BC Cancer Agency Library; staff of the Vancouver Public Library, the Port Moody Library, the North Vancouver District Library and the Port Moody Museum. Gordon Burr, Senior Archivist, and Andra Syvanen of McGill University Archives provided confirmation of Dr Trapp's time at McGill.

Additional photographs were provided by Rick Joyce, Nancy Dilay, Lucy Godwin and Eric Higgs. Robert Thomson of Godwin Books also gave invaluable advice. Ken Smith scanned and organized many of the illustrations.

Relatives and friends have offered personal memories and information about Dr Trapp and her family. Lynn Roseman, a great niece was extremely helpful with information about the family and provided several early photographs. Ray Smith, grandson of Neita Trapp; Nell Lawson, Ethlyn Trapp's niece; Nancy Dilay and Paul Trapp, her great niece and nephew; members of the extended family; and personal friends Betty Lord and Kay Elliot provided valuable input.

Ernest Stelzer designed the book. Patricia Anderson offered valuable advice and professional proofreading. Kate Lautens and the staff of Trafford Publishing gave assistance and printed the book.

Introduction

This book is the story of an extraordinary woman and her father, a British Columbian pioneer.

Dr Ethlyn Trapp was that woman. The first doctor to practice solely using radiation treatment in British Columbia, instrumental in the opening of the British Columbia Cancer Institute, she was well respected at home and abroad. Dr Trapp became the first female president of the British Columbia Medical Association and the National Cancer Institute of Canada. A friend of Emily Carr, a benefactor and humanitarian, she is a British Columbian too little remembered. A world traveller, she gained the respect and friendship of intellectuals, colleagues and children. The purchase of her home, Klee Wyck, on the Capilano River in West Vancouver, was a high point in her life; her subsequent gift of it to the municipality is just one example of her generosity. Never married, a youthful wartime love unfulfilled.

Within seven years of leaving his native England Thomas Trapp, Ethlyn's father, had crossed an ocean and a continent, sailed from California to Alaska, trekked to the interior of British Columbia and crossed the Rockies in winter. He worked as a ditchdigger, prospected for gold, ranched and finally settled into a prosperous business career in New Westminster. In ten years, from the age of forty-five, he fathered four sons and four daughters, one of whom died in infancy. Three boys, all pilots, were killed in the Great War. The eldest son took on the family business, two daughters became doctors and one married a Canadian First World War flying ace.

The family allowed the author to write about these pioneer British Columbians, whose story includes: transcontinental railroads, a gold rush, tough times and murder in the interior of British Columbia, Great War sacrifice, growth of New Westminster, British Columbia's first radiation oncologist, the British Columbia Cancer Institute, a woman at the head of the medical society, friend of Emily Carr, a West Vancouver benefactor and unrequited love hidden for half a century.

It was Ethlyn, the eldest daughter of the family, that led me to write this book and research the Trapp family that came to play such an important role in the burgeoning city of New Westminster.

However, the story begins with her father's journey from Essex to Ontario in the 1870s. That two brothers from a middle-class background in Victorian England should look to seek their fortunes across the seas was not unusual, but it took both good luck and hard work, allied with perseverance, to achieve success. Thomas, the elder of the two, eventually found that success in New Westminster, British Columbia, two decades later. Although he supported his younger brother Samuel and gave him work when he could, the younger did not succeed and died in virtual obscurity in Nelson in his mid-forties.

From Ontario Thomas's odyssey started with a transcontinental rail and sea journey to Victoria, on Vancouver Island, less than a year later and led to a series of adventures that would rival any pioneer's stories. He found work in the fledgling Vancouver but was soon lured into the Cassiar gold rush of 1874–1876. Luckless, he didn't stay long and trekked into the interior to the Nicola Valley to raise livestock before being hired to pack supplies to the railway surveyors planning the trans-Canadian rail route east of the Rockies at Athabasca. A treacherous winter crossing of the Yellowhead Pass to bring ammunition to starving Indians, a close call with a murderous gang near Kamloops in the interior of the province and the severe winter of 1876–1878 brought him back to New Westminster. There, he became a successful businessman operating a store supplying materials and farm goods throughout the Fraser Valley, was a major player in the consortium that opened up the railway system south of the Fraser River, raised a family and was active in a wide range of community endeavours.

The story of the Great War features heavily in the history of the family. Three of four sons were killed as pilots in successive years. A daughter, Neita, married the flying ace Raymond Collishaw, second only to Billy Bishop, but believed by many to be a better flyer. Two surviving Trapp daughters became doctors, Ethlyn rising to the highest levels of her profession and her community.

Dr Ethlyn Trapp was the first woman in the province to seek training in the specialty of radiotherapy and to devote her medical career to its practice and the care of people with cancer. She was one of a small group of physicians who promoted the establishment of the British Columbia Cancer Institute, later to become the internationally recognised British Columbia Cancer Agency. Not only was she forceful in gaining the support of the British Columbia Medical Association and her medical colleagues, she acted as the Institute's Medical Director during the Second World War. When the Institute was strapped for funds, she even offered to donate her own radiotherapy equipment to the clinic. Respected by her colleagues both at home and abroad, during her training in various centres in Europe in the 1930s she established friendships that endured across the years. The respect of physicians and scientists in Canada was demonstrated when she was elected the first female president of the British Columbia Medical Association and the first female president of the National Cancer Institute of Canada. She was the first woman to deliver the annual Osler Lecture in Vancouver.

In her personal life she travelled extensively, made friends wherever she went, was generous, supported arts and international charitable organisations and made her home and garden open to many from across Canada and Europe. She never married but welcomed the children of her family and friends with games and goodies whenever they visited. As the children grew, she encouraged them to read literature of the time supporting women's rights and aspirations. Her interest in the arts was bolstered by her friendship with Emily Carr. Ethlyn had many male friends but there is little hint of romance, although

correspondence suggests that, *"this was not as she would have chosen."*
The source of this phrase in one of her last letters probably lay in the
Balfour Sanatorium just after the Great War some fifty years earlier.

In a world of science and medicine dominated by men until the
middle of the last century, two women preceded Ethlyn in playing a
pioneer role in the treatment of cancer by radiation. In some respects
they were similar and demonstrated what was for women, for at least
the first half of the twentieth century, a remarkable achievement to
gain success in cancer research and treatment. Ethlyn Trapp must
surely have faced a similar male bastion in the growing province of
British Columbia.

Margaret Cleaves (1848–1917), the daughter of a doctor who encouraged her to pursue a medical career, was the first person recorded to
have used radium in the treatment of cancer of the uterus. In 1903
this New York physician described treating a patient with carcinoma
of the cervix in the weekly *New York Medical Record*.[1] In the article
she asked, *"whether radium may not prove a veritable Aladdin's lamp
to medical science...."* Dr Cleaves had borrowed one gram of radium
chloride sealed in a glass tube from Professor Charles Baskerfield
of the chemistry department of the University of North Carolina.
She treated two patients with limited exposure to the substance but
observed marked regression in their tumours before she was obliged
to return the radium source.[2]

At several points in her life, Dr Cleaves suffered what she called a
"sprained brain," and had to take a leave of absence from her work
to recuperate. Dr Cleaves described her experiences in the anony-
mously published *Autobiography of a Neurasthenia*, and attributed
female neurasthenia not simply to overwork, but to woman's ambitions for her intellectual, social, and financial success, ambitions that
could not be accommodated within the structures of late nineteenth-
century society. Nonetheless, she felt, *"women, more than men, are
handicapped at the outset, not necessarily because they are women,
but because, suddenly and without the previous preparations that men
for generations have had, they attempt to fulfill certain conditions and
are expected to qualify themselves for certain work and distinctions."* It

may be true, she conceded, *"that girls and women are unfit to bear the continued labour of mind because of the disqualifications existing in their physiological life."*

Marie Curie (1867–1934), the woman who discovered the radium that Cleaves used, was born Marya Sklodowska in Russian-occupied Poland, the youngest of five children. In her youth and throughout her life, Marya faced nervous problems similar to those of Cleaves. Perhaps these were of similar making in two young women straining to succeed in a male-dominated medical and scientific society. Marya's parents, both teachers, worn down by the Russian occupation of Poland, struggled with oppression and financial hardship. When Marya was ten years of age her mother died of tuberculosis.

Marya was shy and timid. Her efforts in her early education were successful but extracted a heavy toll and, at the age of fifteen, resulted in the first of many *"nervous breakdowns,"* which she referred to as *"the fatigue of growth and study."*[3]

In Russian dominated Poland, girls were denied scientific education and women were not admitted to Warsaw University or any university in the Russian Empire. Marya, as with other like-minded young women, educated themselves in small groups in their homes in defiance of the authorities. In the face of continuing financial hardship Marya chose to work as a governess to help pay for her elder sister's medical studies in Paris. From the age of 18 to 24 she toiled on her sister and family's behalf, often experiencing near breakdowns in her health. Her obligations fulfilled, it was Marya's turn to be supported in her studies at the Sorbonne. Despite her lack of formal education, within three years, through sheer determination and constant study, she received her degree in physics and, furthermore, was top of the class. A year later she earned a degree in mathematics, though on this occasion only came second in the class!

Once in Paris, she chose to use the French spelling of her name and became Marie. Married to the physicist Pierre Curie, she toiled alongside him to discover Radium, an achievement that was announced to the world on December 26, 1898. The story of Marie's extraction of pure radium from several tons of Austrian ore is well known. By 1902 she had separated 0.1 grams of radium and determined its atomic weight. It was recognized that as radioactivity is given off, an element changes. Uranium "decays" to radium and eventually to lead. One of the decay products of radium is the gas radon. Collecting and using the gas, called emanation, could keep the precious and rare radium as a permanent source of radiation. At first the gas was collected in fine glass tubes.

It was most surely similar tubes that were used by Margaret Cleaves and others in their first groundbreaking treatments of cancer sufferers.

Dr Ethlyn Trapp was the first woman to rise to prominence in cancer care in British Columbia at a time when medicine was still a male domain. She came to medicine in her mid-thirties and no doubt, as for women elsewhere in the world, she endured pressures, seeking to succeed in the male-dominated profession in British Columbia. Ethlyn Trapp suffered a severe leg injury as a child, causing her to endure a limp throughout life, but there is no evidence of the "nervous problems" that plagued Cleaves and Curie.

Suffering the loss of three brothers in the First World War and working in a military hospital left little time for worrying about her own situation. After medical school she worked first as a paediatrician but, impressed with the work of Dr Prowd at St Paul's Hospital in Vancouver, she determined to study radiotherapy. While studying in Germany, Scandinavia and England, Ethlyn demonstrated a sense of purpose that helped ensure her sound training, while her personality won her many lifelong friends.

Dr Trapp opened the way for many other women to play important roles in treatment of and research into cancer diseases in the latter part of the twentieth century.

It was the life of Dr Trapp, not just her professional career, but her remarkable personal life that led me to write about her. The book is in no way a medical treatise and there are very few technical terms. The book is about a pioneer family in the late nineteenth and early twentieth centuries, and the life, personality and achievements of a woman who gained prominence without the lasting attention that she deserves.

Late in her life, in notes prepared for a final letter to a First World War veteran she had nursed in the Balfour Sanatorium, she wrote words which will forever lead to conjecture as to their true meaning: *My life has been a fortunate one in so many ways—though not as I would have chosen.*

Trapp Family Tree

Possible early member. John Trapp (1762)
First Waltham Abbey member of Parliament from Woodward, Essex

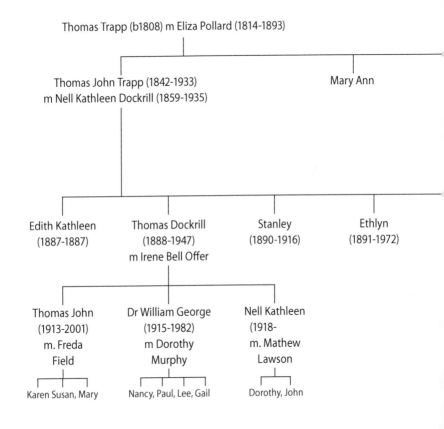

Thomas Trapp (b1808) m Eliza Pollard (1814-1893)

Thomas John Trapp (1842-1933)
m Nell Kathleen Dockrill (1859-1935)

Mary Ann

Edith Kathleen
(1887-1887)

Thomas Dockrill
(1888-1947)
m Irene Bell Offer

Stanley
(1890-1916)

Ethlyn
(1891-1972)

Thomas John
(1913-2001)
m. Freda
Field

Dr William George
(1915-1982)
m Dorothy
Murphy

Nell Kathleen
(1918-
m. Mathew
Lawson

Karen Susan, Mary

Nancy, Paul, Lee, Gail

Dorothy, John

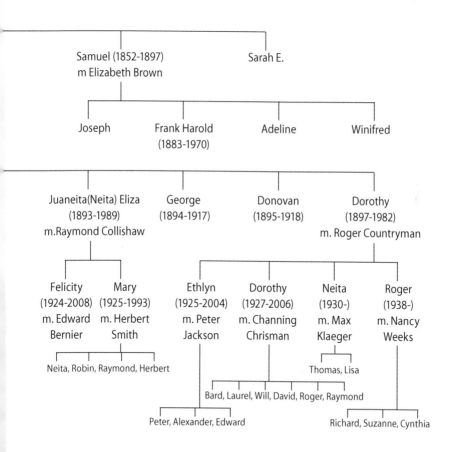

Samuel (1852-1897)
m Elizabeth Brown

Sarah E.

Joseph   Frank Harold   Adeline   Winifred
           (1883-1970)

Juaneita(Neita) Eliza   George   Donovan   Dorothy
(1893-1989)   (1894-1917)   (1895-1918)   (1897-1982)
m.Raymond Collishaw   m. Roger Countryman

Felicity   Mary   Ethlyn   Dorothy   Neita   Roger
(1924-2008)   (1925-1993)   (1925-2004)   (1927-2006)   (1930-)   (1938-)
m. Edward   m. Herbert   m. Peter   m. Channing   m. Max   m. Nancy
Bernier   Smith   Jackson   Chrisman   Klaeger   Weeks

Neita, Robin, Raymond, Herbert   Thomas, Lisa

Bard, Laurel, Will, David, Roger, Raymond

Peter, Alexander, Edward   Richard, Suzanne, Cynthia

Chronology of Dr Ethlyn Trapp

July 18, 1891	Born, New Westminster
1900–1909	All Hallows School, Yale
1909–1910	McGill University College, Vancouver
1910–1913	McGill University, Montreal: Graduated BA
1914–1920	Occupational therapist, Vancouver & Balfour
1920–1923	Travel, South East Asia
1924–1927	McGill University Montreal: Graduated MD, CM
1927	Part of the year in Edinburgh
1927–1929	Intern, Montreal & Vancouver
	Assistant Surgeon, Hawaii
1929–1930	Postgraduate medicine & surgery, Vienna, Berlin
1930–1932	General Practice, New Westminster
1932–1933	Postgraduate radiotherapy, Vienna, Stockholm & London
1933–1935	Assistant, radiation therapy, St Paul's Vancouver
1935–1937	European study, Brussels, Berlin, Frankfurt, Paris, Stockholm, London & Manchester
1937–1940	Private practice, Vancouver
1940–1943	Acting medical superintendent, BC Cancer Institute
1943–1945	Medical Director, BC Cancer Institute
1945–1960	Private practice, Vancouver
1919, 1939–1941, 1970	Meetings and correspondence with George Godwin
1938–1943	Visits and correspondence with Emily Carr
1945	President of the BC Medical Association
1952	President of the National Cancer Institute of Canada
1952	Osler lecturer, Vancouver
1954	Honorary Doctor of Science, UBC
1954	Honorary Fellowship, Faculty of Radiologists, UK
1968	Order of Canada
1940	Purchased Klee Wyck, West Vancouver
1959	Klee Wyck given to West Vancouver
July 31, 1972	Died, West Vancouver

Dates in *italics* are less certain

Thomas John Trapp
A Father's Tale

At the time of the "Great Fire" of New Westminster in 1898, Thomas John Trapp was already a prosperous and influential figure in the life of the burgeoning city; but how had he achieved this position?

The story of his pioneering life as a young immigrant from England a quarter of a century earlier is remarkable, though not unlike that of others who came to British Columbia in search of a new life. Did he relate some of his adventures to his children seated around the fire in the family living room on cold and rainy winter evenings? We know he wrote a journal that was later donated to the Kamloops Museum Archives and from which his grandson, Thomas John, described his journey from England.[4]

Thomas John Trapp, the son of a Baptist forest ranger working for Sir Heribwald Wake, was born on June 4, 1842, in Waltham Abbey, Essex. Thomas John grew up in the town where his father, Thomas Trapp, was also the town surveyor, and began work as a clerk in a grocery store. Later he became a commercial salesman for a wholesale pharmaceutical manufacturer in London.

At the age of thirty, Thomas, along with his brother Samuel, left Essex to come to Canada, and in his journal he wrote:

October 4th 1872. Friday. Dear Mother called Bro. Sam and myself about 5.30 am. Got up at once and finished packing Boxes. Had Breakfast and after bidding good bye to dear Father, Mother & Sister Pollie, who were rather cut up by our leaving, but on the whole bore up wonderfully, we walked to Waltham Station and caught the 7.59 Train to London.

From London, the brothers took the train to Liverpool and embarked for Canada on the Steam Ship Missipia of the Dominion Line. The voyage was long and uncomfortable and the food bad. It was ten days before landfall, and a further two weeks before they were able to disembark. Fog marred the trip at both ends and in mid-ocean the waves were high enough to wash across the ship amidships. They landed at Point Levi(s) across from Quebec City and received train passes to continue their journey. They failed to find work in Montreal or Toronto because *"immigration was outstripping job opportunities."*

Thomas settled at first in St Thomas, Ontario. His initial work was as a day labourer, wielding pick and shovel in the construction of the Canada Southern Railroad, while Samuel found work in London. Thomas was paid $1.75 for a ten-hour day. The railroad ran from Buffalo to Detroit on the northern shore of Lake Erie with St Thomas about half way between the two. The railroad desperately needed to reach Chicago to create a bridge line between New York State and railroads in the Western United States. By 1873 the Chicago & Canada Southern Railroad had crossed the Detroit River by ferryboat from Gordon, Ontario, to Stoney Island, a 900-foot trestle to Gross Ile, and a 1400-foot bridge with double-draw section to the Michigan mainland.

That was as far as the railroad ever reached. All this new construction had brought about a heavy financial drain on the railroad and when it suspended payments on its bonds, Cornelius Vanderbilt stepped in and paid off the creditors. In doing so, he gained control of the Canada Southern and its subsidiary, the Chicago & Canada Southern, opening the way to Chicago. With the railroad work at an end, Thomas found employment in a general store but, being restless, looked west to British Columbia and Victoria, where he arrived on April 23, 1873. The trans-Canada Canadian Pacific Railroad was not completed until the driving of the last spike at Craigellachie in British Columbia twelve years later. So to go west Thomas used the newly created American transcontinental route from Chicago to Omaha, Nebraska, and Sacramento, California.

The 1860s and 70s were dramatic times in the building of multiple separate railroads in America, which gradually amalgamated or were absorbed in the race to produce a transcontinental railroad. The American Pacific Railroad Act, passed on June 24, 1862, provided for the construction of a transcontinental route from an unspecified point on the Missouri River to a western terminus at Sacramento or San Francisco. On November 17, 1863, Abraham Lincoln declared that Omaha would be the eastern terminus of the new transcontinental railroad. Two years later the first locomotive, the *General Sherman*, of Civil War fame, arrived in Omaha from Chicago. The Union Pacific Railroad had begun construction from Omaha, Nebraska, in 1863, while the Central Pacific broke ground at Sacramento. The two lines met at Promontory Point, Utah, and on May 10, 1869, a golden spike joined the two railways, thus completing North America's first trans-continental railroad, just in time for the likes of Thomas Trapp to cut days off his journey west to the Pacific Coast.

Gretchen Schafer's diary, posted on the web site of the Central Pacific Railroad Photographic History Museum,[5] describes a journey from Chicago to San Francisco on the way to Olympia, Washington Territory, in November 1871. Her train journey via Omaha and Sacra-mento took eight days and ended with a steamer trip from Oakland to San Francisco. She continued by sea to Victoria, a voyage Trapp emulated two years later, although his train journey was probably completed in only two or possibly three days. Train travel was pleas-antly casual in those days. Trapp's journal relates how, when the train stopped for water at a creek in the Sierra Nevada, he left his cap there. The conductor obligingly stopped the train and waited while Thomas ran back about a mile to retrieve the cap. From his diary it seemed a carefree journey: "*We rode on the top of Cars the greater part of the day, and had plenty of fun with the Girls our Fellow Passengers.*" From San Francisco he sailed to Victoria on the Prince Albert.

Low Standards of Morality

In 1873 Thomas John crossed from Victoria to New Westminster on the Hudson's Bay Company's sternwheeler *Enterprise*. An alternative would have been the side-wheeler *Wilson G. Hunt*, operated by John Irving, son of the veteran steamer operator and New Westminster pioneer Captain William Irving. The route from Victoria to New Westminster and then up the Fraser River had been popularized during the gold rush of 1858. Competition between the two vessels was fierce, forcing bargain prices in the 1870s, of which Thomas would have taken advantage. The competition was resolved in 1880 when the two companies agreed to cooperate. The Hudson's Bay Company operated the *Olympia*, renamed the *Princess Louise*, to New Westminster from Victoria and maintained the mail contract for the route. Irving provided a connecting service with one of his river steamers from New Westminster to Yale in what became known as the *"arf and arf"* arrangement.[6]

From New Westminster, Thomas hiked the trail to the Burrard Inlet and then to the Hastings Sawmill. Within two weeks he found a job loading a ship with spars for three dollars a day and bunked with the sailors. Stamp's Mill, bought by Heatley of London, had become Hastings Sawmill Co. in 1870. The first school in what was to become Vancouver was a private school built by the Hastings Sawmill in 1872. The school's first teacher was the *"young and pretty"* Georgia Sweeney, daughter of a machinist at the mill, hired for $40 a month. The school had a wood stove and, at one point, an organ for singsongs.[7]

Restless as ever, and unhappy with the *"low standards of morality at the mills and wharves,"* Trapp left to return to Victoria where he dug ditches and cut cordwood at Spring Ridge. Spring Ridge ran approximately west to east about a mile from the shoreline. It was the site of Victoria's original public spring near to the intersection of Denman and Spring Street. Governor Douglas had called it Fountain Spring. In the 1860s, horse-drawn carts of the Spring Ridge Water Co. carved trails along the ridge to Chambers Street and into town. This was also the site of the Empire Brewery and Saloon (1885), which used the spring water to brew beer. Spring Ridge School was built in 1887 at the corner of Chambers and Gladstone and demolished in 1968 to provide a parking lot for Victoria High School.

For cutting cordwood Trapp was paid $1.25 per cord for dry wood and $1.00 for green wood. He was next employed in the dry goods store of A. B. Gray at $40 a month, soon raised to $75. Now that he was more settled, he was pleased to attend St Andrew's Presbyterian Church twice on Sundays, but this contented state was not to last long.

Gold Rush Fever

Following the findings of Angus McCullock and Henry Thibert in 1873, the Cassiar gold rush, from 1874 to 1876, brought a flood of miners up the Stikine River en route to the Dease Lake area of northern British Columbia. A participant in that flood of hopefuls was Thomas Trapp.

The same John Irving, whose ships transported people from Victoria to New Westminster, also had ships sailing to Alaska, and probably to Ketchikan or Wrangell at the mouth of the Stikine River. Irving went so far as to have a sternwheeler, the *Glenora*, built for service on the river. However, he negotiated an agreement with his competitors to share profits of the Stikine run in exchange for withdrawing his vessel and returning to the Fraser River.[8] As the Cassiar gold rush got underway in 1874, members of the Stikine Nation began freighting cargo up the river in big canoes, both for wages and on a contract basis. One account states Indians were freighting for $30 per weight-ton, while the steamers, when they operated, charged $40 per measurement-ton.[9]

It is almost certain that Trapp took the same route in the spring of 1874, but how far he progressed up the Stikine River, or whether he reached the Dease Lake area, we don't know. We do know that he had no success, returning to Victoria and then travelling again into the Interior of the province where he became involved in the cattle business at Kamloops and in the Nicola Valley. In the Kamloops voters list of 1876 he was listed as *"stock raiser of Napier Lake."*

The Overland Railway

At the time Trapp ventured into the interior of the province, there was great surveying activity in search of the best route for the railway to take through the mountains. Completion of the coast-to-coast railroad had been promised to British Columbia as part of its deal to enter into confederation with Canada. British Columbia's first Lieutenant-Governor, Joseph Trutch, approached Walter Moberly, the civil engineer, to organize survey crews to work in the Revelstoke and Golden area. In his early career Moberly had laid out the streets of New Westminster and in 1865 had discovered Eagle Pass between Shuswap Lake in the North Okanagan and the Columbia River near present day Revelstoke. He was already convinced that this would be the ideal route for the railway and had blazed a tree in the pass with the words *"This is the Pass of the Overland Railway."* Moberly was very unhappy when his boss, Sandford Fleming, the Chief Engineer for the transcontinental railway project, ordered him to relocate his crews north to the Yellowhead Pass.[10]

The Chief Engineer, later Sir Sandford Fleming, like others involved in the American and Canadian transcontinental railways, could not plan timetables because every district, city, state or province had its own time of day. Greenwich Mean Time (GMT) had been established in the nineteenth century for British maritime navigation. Fleming proposed that 24 time zones should be created every 15 degrees of longitude around the world starting with the prime meridian through Greenwich. The railroads began to use the system on November 18, 1883. A Meridian Conference of twenty-seven nations, held in Washington DC in 1884, approved the proposal in principle, although it was not established in law until the beginning of the twentieth century.[11]

Trapp, now in the Kamloops region, was employed to take a pack train of supplies to the surveyors working in the Yellowhead Pass area. Walter Moberly had established the Athabasca Depot close to present day Jasper but, disillusioned by Fleming's rejection of his southerly route, he and the surveyors had left and gone east by the time Trapp arrived.

The journey that Trapp took in the summer and fall of 1876 up the North Thompson River to Tete Jaune Cache, and across the Yellowhead Pass to winter at the Athabasca Depot, is told in a series of articles housed in the Kamloops Museum and Archives. Mary Balf compiled these articles from Trapp's journal, which was given to the Museum by his daughter Ethlyn. The following accounts lend vivid descriptions of the hazards and trials of pioneer life of the time.

The year 1876 was a bad one for unseasonably cold and wet summer weather with high-river and flooding conditions reaching a peak in July, making the journey very difficult. About a dozen people left Kamloops on June 22. Battling the weather and mosquitoes, it was July 7 before they reached Raft River, the present day Clearwater. Much of the journey had been made by flat-bottom sternwheeler that unloaded supplies at the Raft River Cache and returned to Kamloops. While waiting for the steamer to return, Trapp did some hunting and *shot groundhog and skunk, no sign of bear or deer.*" A week later they were at Vavenby, and shortly after at "Round Prairie," the site of present day Avola. The next two weeks proved heavy going through Blue River and Little Hells Gate before they reached Albreda on Sunday, August 6: "*A horrible journey through mud and holes, very trying on the horses it also being very wet and uncomfortable. Made a large fire in front of the tent.*" Two days later Trapp reported that it was "*very cold, snow having fallen pretty heavily on the ground after heavy rain.*" August 19, two months after leaving Kamloops, the group reached Tete Jaune Cache.

Tete Jaune Cache, the Yellowhead Highway and Yellowhead Pass were named after a fur trader and trapper that guided for the Hudson's Bay Company (HBC) in the early 1800s. The yellow-haired Iroquois Metis guide, Pierre Hastination (or Pierre Bostonais), was named

Tete Jaune by the French voyageurs because of his blonde-streaked hair. Tete Jaune led an HBC group across the Rocky Mountains in December 1819, to meet and befriend the Shuswap Indians. He established a fur cache on the Grand Fork of the Fraser and relocated his cache in 1827 to the vicinity of the Shuswap salmon fishing camp on the Fraser River, where the town of Tete Jaune stands today. A year later, near the headwaters of the Smoky River, Tete Jaune, his brother, their wives and children were murdered by the Beaver Indians for revenge on the Iroquois people for their earlier encroachment into the Beaver's hunting territory.[12]

Trapp recorded in his journal, *"Reached Tete Jaune Cache at 10 am. All well. Crossed cargo in canoe and swam horses. Washed clothes. Went down to Cache and read papers, had dinner and went up river to see and fish river. B.M. here 2441 feet above S.L."* He then set out on the trek over the Yellowhead, which took eight days. *"Road very rocky, crossed the Miette River many times, some of the crossings very bad. Dan saw black bear and chased him with an axe, but could not come up with him."*

On August 30, the party reached Athabasca Depot, located in Henry House near the confluence of the Miette and Athabasca Rivers on the outskirts of present day Jasper. When Trapp arrived, he found that both Henry House and Jasper House were deserted. Moberley, fed up with the decision to choose the Yellowhead as the likely rail crossing, had packed up his survey crew and left. He moved to Manitoba and turned to independent engineering.

William Henry had established the first permanent settlement in the Jasper area in the winter of 1810–11 at Old Fire Point just below the present site of the Fairmont Jasper Park Lodge. David Thompson, the noted explorer, had left Henry there while he and his companions opened a trail over the Athabasca Pass to the Bow Valley. Two years later the rival to the HBC, the North West Company, established Jasper House named after Jasper Hawes, a long time company clerk. Jasper House was located at the south end of Brule Lake near the mining town of Pocahontas but moved to Jasper Lake, a seasonal widening of the Athabasca River close to Jasper, in 1829. The post was closed in 1884.

The exact location of Henry House is not known but it must have been on the eastern shore of the Athabasca River. The Indians and fur traders who brought their goods to trade there could graze their animals on a flat piece of land known to this day as Henry House Flats close to the Lodge Road approach to Jasper Park Lodge. Trapp and his colleagues ferried the supplies across the river on rafts and stored them at Henry House. The cattle and horses were taken to winter beside the Bow River.

H. A. F. McLeod, in charge of the Eastern Division of railway surveying, asked John Glassey to arrange for Trapp to take control of the Athabasca Depot and stay over the winter of 1876 at Henry House, with Michael O'Keefe as his assistant. The pair settled into a routine with Banjo, their faithful canine companion. They made friends with several Indians, notably Pierre and his wife Marie, baked

Fig 1. Henry House Flats. Photograph taken in 1915 shows the wide area available to graze horses and for the Indians to trade. (Image courtesy of M. P. Bridgland. Digital image, copyright 2000, University of Alberta and E. S. Higgs, University of Alberta)

bread regularly, did occasional laundry, cleaned their guns and read Spurgeon's sermons on Sundays. Trapp refers to Spurgeon frequently in his journal.

Charles Haddon Spurgeon was the most widely popular of English preachers in the nineteenth century. He was born in Kelvedon, Essex, England, on June 19, 1834. At the age of nineteen he was installed as minister of the New Park Street Chapel, Southwark, London, later to become the Metropolitan Tabernacle. Spurgeon published his first sermon in January 1855, a practice that would continue until 1916, twenty-four years after his death. Spurgeon ministered to a congregation of almost 6,000 people each Sunday, published his sermons weekly, wrote a monthly magazine, and founded a college for pastors, two orphanages, an old-folks home, a colportage society to distribute bibles, and several mission stations. Criticized in his later years, his sermons are once more gaining in popularity more than 150 years later.

In his journal Trapp recorded, "*Donald Graham and cook from pack train came to depot for beans and syrup. I also got an exchange of axes from these boys. With Marshall and Charlie cleaning out houses and mudding same. Fixed up chimney of officer's quarters. Louie Campbell and his brother Paulett came with some fresh meat and some bear grease, which we traded for some tea and an old axe and some flour for 6 pairs of moccasins.*"

Major difficulties in the area included crossing the Athabasca River, which had to be achieved using rafts that they built from local timber or even parts of the buildings. Hunting was made difficult by "*a great deal of trouble from, wolves, wolverine and kioties.*" As Christmas approached, things looked bleak. Trapp described Christmas Day: "*Up in good time. Baked a loaf of bread, made dumplings, and currant cake, but badly off for meat, and should have been confined to bacon and beans had not Pierre brought in the leg of a beaver. Gave Pierre and Marie their dinner and a little flour, currants, and one tin of Bake Powder for meat.*"

Snow Rabbit to the Rescue

Early in January, Trapp set off to cross the Yellowhead Pass to Tete Jaune Cache. Most accounts of the trip describe it as a heroic journey to obtain ammunition to save the Indians from starvation. However, Trapp's journal suggests a different slant. Indeed, they were short of ammunition, but it was mail in addition to ammunition that he and Pierre left to collect from Tete Jaune Cache. Pierre and Paulett, both half-breed Iroquois Indians, and three dogs left with Trapp, *"packing blankets etc."*

Travelling was extremely difficult through deep snow; it was soft and the going hard. They ran short of food and Pierre was exhausted. Trapp wrote: *"Then we were 25 miles from the next cache, and barely*

Fig 2. Serene summer at Trapp Lake. No hint of the hardships and near death of the times. (Trapp Lake photo credit to Rick Joyce, Kamloops, BC)

enough food for supper, and 3'6" snow beside. Pierre in evening made a snow rabbit [a spiritual offering] and set him out on the snow, telling him to fetch cold and hard snow, so that we could get to our destination without suffering. Here we had to make the dogs do without supper, and divided it amongst ourselves. For breakfast next morning the halfbreeds cooked bacon rind, and eating it with relish."

The snow rabbit was answered. Cold weather and hard crisp snow conditions returned the next day, and they managed to reach Tete Jaune Cache. They rested three days and undertook the return journey, again under trying conditions, but without the need of spiritual influence. Fourteen days after leaving, they were back at Henry House: *"Settled up with Pierre and Paulett, giving each one cup of shot, gun powder, one box 100 caps, and a little flour and beans, and to Pierre one pair pants, $4.50, and one file."*

Here the journal ends but it is known that Trapp and O'Keefe stayed at the depot until the survey crews returned in the late spring. Trapp made the journey back to his Nicola ranch in September 1877. Trapp Lake was named in record of his stay in the area.

Murder in the Interior

Two years later, in December 1879, Thomas Trapp came close to death in the murder of the Government Agent John Ushher and a shepherd, Kelly, in the Nicola Valley. There are many versions in the telling of the murder. One rendition suggested that the murders were carried out in an Indian uprising. However, what is almost certainly the true account was written the week after, on December 30, by John Tait, the Hudson's Bay Company (HBC) Factor at Kamloops, who told a much different story.[13]

In Tait's account, the blame is laid at the feet of four local vagabonds and thieves, Allen, Charles and Archie McLean and Alexander Hare. The McLean boys' mother was the daughter of Chief Louie of the Kamloops Indians. Their father, Donald McLean of the HBC, was notorious for his dealings with the Indians. No one was surprised when he was murdered in the Chilcotin. The brothers led troubled lives. Prior to the murders, the Government had offered a reward of $250 for their capture and Tait had matched the same amount, though he wrote: *"I took the responsibility of increasing the reward and if not acknowledged by the Company to pay it myself."* The money brought together a group of men as a posse, but John Ushher thought he could bring them in by himself. Tait urged him to take others along but Ushher was confident, saying: *"Don't you be afraid, if I get my eyes on them, they will be sure to come along."* When Ushher did come across them, he dismounted, leaving his pistol on the saddle, and walked towards Hare, putting a hand on his shoulder. Whereupon, Hare promptly threw Ushher to the ground, beat him with his pistol butt and slashed him with a knife. Archie McLean shot Ushher through the skull just above the left eye. Not satisfied with killing, the thugs stole his boots, overcoat, gloves, horse and saddle.

The vagabonds then rode towards Nicola, stopping at Trapp's cabin where they demanded his rifle, shotgun and all the ammunition he had, while two of them held their guns at his head. They left without harming him but met the shepherd Kelly a mile or two down the road and, after a few words, shot him dead. They continued to Douglas Lake, stealing from others but without further killings. At Douglas Lake they tried to urge the local Indians to join them, but they refused. When news of the murders became known, a group of fifteen men from Cache Creek and others from the Kamloops area were gathered and, despite lack of ammunition and severe winter weather, the villains were captured. Eventually the four were hanged in the New Westminster jail. Thomas Trapp gave evidence at their trial.

New Westminster

In the severe weather Trapp lost most of his livestock and, perhaps because of advice from Moberly, Thomas moved to New Westminster with his brother, Samuel. Samuel was ten years Thomas's junior. The two of them worked for the dry goods store R. W. Deane & Company in the early 1880s. They bought out the Deane brothers and renamed it T. J. Trapp & Company. The business was soon successful, selling everything from Singer sewing machines to heavy farm equipment. The store supplied farm machinery to communities throughout the Fraser Valley and as far away as the Okanagan.

Although the business was successful, perhaps there were tensions between the brothers, for we next hear of a Samuel Trapp in Nanaimo in the early 1890s, living with his wife Elizabeth (Brown) and three children in a one-roomed wooden house. Samuel died in 1897 in Nelson, British Columbia, on or about September 1, of "congestion of the lungs," his occupation listed as "dyer" on the death certificate.

Fig 3. The Laurie Bugle, 1884. The bearded Private T. J. Trapp stands at the left of the group with a McLaughlin carriage in the background. The New Westminster team won the annual competition at the prize meeting of the British Columbia Rifle Association. (City of Vancouver Archives, MilP251N93)

The eldest of his three children was Frank Harold, born in 1893. After Samuel died, Frank was taken in as one of the family by his uncle Thomas in New Westminster. Frank later played a major role in Trapp family business on Vancouver Island. Frank died in 1970 and is buried in the Trapp family grave in New Westminster in the Fraser View Cemetery overlooking the river.

Within four years of returning to the coast, Trapp was a member of the victorious New Westminster team that took part in the annual British Columbia Rifle Association competition for the "Laurie Bugle." Major-General J. Wimburn Laurie had presented the silver bugle in 1881 for annual competition between teams of officers and men from Victoria, New Westminster and Nanaimo. In 1884, the bearded Private T. J. Trapp (of T. J. Trapp & Co) was photographed as a member of the New Westminster team that defeated Victoria. His team had 422 successful shots out of 750, compared to 373 by the Victoria team.

One of Trapp's business franchises included selling McLaughlin Carriages. Thomas Trapp loved horses, which may explain his investing in the carriage business. Robert McLaughlin, of carriage fame, founded the McLaughlin Carriage Works in 1869 in Ontario. By 1900 he employed over 600 workmen and had an annual output of 25,000 vehicles. The advent of the automobile at the turn of the century led McLaughlin's to form a motorcar company in 1907 and to begin production of the McLaughlin-Buick. By 1915, sales of carriages were in such decline, that the carriage company was sold to a competitor. After that date, production of McLaughlin carriages was discontinued.

Almost certainly the McLaughlin carriage was the usual mode of transport for the Trapp family through the first years of the 1900s. Trapp wanted nothing to do with the McLaughlin-Buick car when it was introduced. His eldest son, Thomas Dockrill Trapp (T. D.) later reported, *"He always said he preferred his horses because he knew a horse would always get him home."* But T. D. eventually talked him into selling cars, which made the family business the oldest General Motors dealership in Western Canada.

It was one of Trapp's cars that was almost used as a getaway vehicle for one of the biggest bank robberies in North America. Thieves broke into the Bank of Montreal on Columbia Street in New Westminster overnight on September 15, 1911. Their entry was made easier by the night watchman at the bank having taken the evening off to attend a local dance. The thieves ran to Trapp's garage, silently pushed his car out and attempted to start it further down the road. What they didn't know was that Trapp's son had removed the spark plugs so it couldn't start.[14]

In July 1886 Thomas visited Joseph Dockrill on his property on the North Shore of the Burrard Inlet, opposite present day Port Moody. Dockrill was of Irish descent and had farmed in Ontario with his father before coming west in August 1883. He had settled on a parcel of land on the Admiralty Reserve named "Sunnyside." The Reserve was close to present day Ioco, with Mossom Creek running though

Fig 4. A gathering at Prospect Point (circa 1890s). Many people were brought by McLaughlin carriages, perhaps some of them purchased from Thomas Trapp. (Photographer, Richard H. Trueman, City of Vancouver Archives LGN 473)

it. Joseph later set up a sawmill on the creek. The Reserve had been used by the Royal Navy for cannon firing practice from their "Man of War" ships moored in the Inlet. Joseph had four daughters, all schoolteachers, and one of them, Nellie, followed her father to British Columbia to keep house for him. Life was not easy—she later recalled serving Christmas turkey on a shingle for want of a platter.

It is not known why Thomas Trapp had travelled from New Westminster for the visit. It may have been to join the crowds who had gone to see the first transcontinental train arrive from Eastern Canada.

The famous rail journey from Montreal had taken five days and nineteen hours to travel 4,650 kilometres, arriving in Port Moody on July 4, 1886, one minute behind schedule. Trapp later described the event: "*The day, a Sunday, dawned bright and warm, and the little settlement was in a festive mood. Excursion boats arrived from Victoria and Nanaimo. Friends and relatives came to visit us from other places. Down the inlet from Vancouver came several families in their little boats. After the speeches we all returned home.*"[15]

To visit Dockrill, Trapp would have travelled on horseback, or possibly by carriage, from New Westminster along North Road to Aliceville at the western end of Port Moody, site of the present day Andres Winery. As a young girl, his daughter Ethlyn would have been taken by her parents along the same route to catch the train to take her to school in Yale. North Road had been built by the

Fig 5. Nellie Dockrill, later Nelle or Nell Trapp. (Photograph from the *Lougheed Mall Discover*, Spring 1991)

Fig 6. The arrival of Sir John A. Macdonald and Lady Macdonald at Port Moody on July 24, 1886. Nellie Dockrill in the tipped white hat, seen centred below the principals on the train, stands with Thomas, the man she would marry a month or two later. (City of Vancouver Archives, CanP62N39)

Royal Engineers in a direct line from their depot at Sapperton just upstream from New Westminster on the Fraser River to the Burrard Inlet to provide winter access to ocean waters, should the Fraser River freeze up as it had from time to time. On reaching the shores of the inlet, Thomas would then have crossed to Sunnyside in a rowboat.

Trapp returned to Sunnyside later in the month to meet the train carrying Sir John A. and Lady Macdonald. Perhaps he had already "set his cap" at Nelle because she accompanied him to the event. Lady Agnes Macdonald was so fascinated by the scenery of the Rocky Mountains that she wrote that she had a candlebox (an empty candle-box) fastened to the platform of the cowcatcher in front of the loco-motive and sat there for the last 600 miles of the journey. She arrived in Port Moody *"healthy looking and badly tanned"* and remarked, *"I must bid good-bye to candlebox and cowcatcher, and content myself with an easy chair on the deck of a steamer bound for Victoria."*[16]

Sunnyside became a popular family retreat for members of the Trapp and Dockrill families. The property, divided into ten parcels, remains in the family as Sunnyside Properties, straddling Mossom Creek, with the sand bar called Dockrill Point reaching out into the inlet at low tide.

The Great Fire

L ike another blaze that had destroyed much of Vancouver, the "Great Fire" of New Westminster was devastating.[17] It began in hay stored on the wharf by Front Street at 11.00 PM on Saturday, September 10, 1898. The warehouse was soon ablaze and the fire spread to the City Market. The accounting records of the market were saved but the flames spread rapidly, fanned by a strong northeasterly wind. Matters were made worse when three sternwheelers, the *Gladys*, *Edgar* and *Bon Accord*, caught fire and were cut adrift from the wharf

Fig 7. Aftermath of the Great Fire. Within two days of the fire of September 10, 1898, Thomas Trapp, standing on the right of the line of dignitaries, had reopened his store on Front Street in downtown New Westminster. William Hunter, bookkeeper for the City Market and presumably the one responsible for rescuing the Market's books, is on the extreme left of the picture. (City of Vancouver Archives, OutP263N103)

in a strong ebb tide, setting fire to more hay stores. The fire spread across Front and Columbia Streets, threatening all properties below Agnes Street.

Within a week of the Great Fire, businesses were operating in temporary quarters. The fire losses were assessed at $2.5 million. The photograph in Figure 7 shows Trapp and others in front of his store some 48 hours after the fire. The position of the store, close by the rail tracks, suggests that it had been located on Front Street.

The No. 1 Fire Hall, a wooden building, was consumed, as were the YMCA and the Public Library. Reinforcements recruited from the Vancouver Fire Department, as well as the fire pump on the local ferry, finally contained the fire. Much of the city was destroyed from Royal Avenue to the river, apart from some brick buildings.

For a further twenty years after the fire of 1898, fire fighting in New Westminster continued to rely on horse-drawn fire engines. Each fire engine had three horses, one driver, one captain and one or more hose men. On receiving an alarm, the horses were trained to go directly to their position at the front of the fire engine. Once in position, the harness, which was suspended from the ceiling was dropped onto their backs and the collars automatically connected. The driver assumed his place on the engine and the hose men checked the reins and harness connections to make sure the engine was properly attached. The driver had the responsibility of tending to the horses during his time on shift, and would exercise them at least once a day by riding them throughout the city streets surrounding the fire hall.

The Fraser River Crossings

As youngsters, Thomas's children would have looked down from the family home on Agnes Street to the river below and watched the busy traffic and the ferry as it crossed the river from Brownsville on the southern shore in South Westminster.

Brownsville was the terminus of the New Westminster Southern Railway, which ran from opposite the city centre of New Westminster to Hazelmere. Brownsville Bar, a small park, lies today between the Pattullo Bridge and the Sky Train Bridge.

Just below the Sky Train Bridge, Old Yale Road ends at a small private wharf. This was the site from which Ferries transported people and goods from the New Westminster Southern Railway (NWSR), which opened in 1891, and the area known as South Westminster across the river to New Westminster until the first rail bridge opened in 1904. Thomas Trapp played an important role in the consortium that built the railway, acting as its secretary. A. J. McColl, a New Westminster barrister and another principal of the NWSR, owned the brickyard along Parsons Channel and other lots at Port Kells, as well as those at the railway's terminus in South Westminster. Other principals, members of the New Westminster Board of Trade, included Judge W. Norman Bole, Henry Hoy (a contractor), Gordon Edward Corbould (a barrister), Alexander Ewen (noted salmon canner), and John Hendry,

Fig 8. The Brownsville Ferry Slip (circa 1902) at the foot of Old Yale Road located between the present day Sky Train and Patullo Bridges next to the small Brownsville Park. (City of Surrey Archives 180.6.01)

president of the BC Mills, Timber & Trading Company (RCPM Co.), the Great Northern Railway's front man in British Columbia.

The ferry that the children would have watched from their home on Agnes Street above the New Westminster wharfs was an improvement on the first ferry, known as the "K de K" (*Knivet de Knivet*). In 1890, to enhance connection with the upcoming railway, the New Westminster Board of Trade replaced the old ferry with an improved version, the *Surrey*. The children might have appreciated the sight of the K de K and its motley cargo more than its more modern replacement.

Knivet is an ancient English family name of significance. Sir John Knivet was the Lord Chief Justice of England and Wales from 1365–

Fig 9. The Ferry K de K operating between Surrey and New Westminster in 1884. (City of Surrey Archives, 209.03)

1372. However, other spellings of the name with famous connections are known. The ferry licence was sublet to Angus Grant of New Westminster who built the ferry and named it after a close friend with the unusual name of Knyvett de Knyvett.[18] New Westminster council named K de K Court in the city after J. S. Knyvett de Knyvett.

Knyvett is also an ancient English name that can be traced back to thirteenth-century Norfolk. Sir Thomas Knyvett foiled the gunpowder plot to blow up London's Houses of Parliament in 1605 when he discovered the gunpowder in the cellars and arrested Guy Fawkes. Perhaps J. S. Knyvett was a man of action, like his ancestor from a long line of Norfolk noblemen.

In the late nineteenth century, railways and their creation were an increasing force in travel and commerce. The New Westminster Southern Railway ran eastward from Brownsville along the southern side of the Fraser River with stops at Liverpool (just east of present day 124th Street), east of which was a parcel of land owned by Trapp, the Secretary of the consortium. Bon Accord (near the Port Mann Bridge) and Port Kells, where the line turned south to Cloverdale and Hazelmere, were additional stops. Initially, Bon Accord was a location where steamboats on their way to Fort Langley and Yale nudged ashore to take on wood and leave mail and supplies. After 1891, Bon Accord developed as a station on the New Westminster and Southern Railway. When the section of railway from Brownsville to Port Kells was sold to the Canadian Northern Pacific railway in 1914—Canadian National (CNR) after 1917—Bon Accord became the link for ferry and barge service to Vancouver Island. However, the CNR found it difficult to compete with the service provided by the Canadian Pacific out of Vancouver Harbour. After the line was purchased by the Canadian Northern the site was renamed Port Mann.[19] It was the only Canadian railway to be built without government subsidy.

Of course it was important for the railway to connect with the United States. This was achieved in 1891 when the New Westminster Southern Railway joined up with the Fairhaven & Southern Railroad Company at Blaine. At the time, Fairhaven was part of present day Bellingham. With the completion of this southern connection, the

Fig 10. Bridging the Fraser. The New Westminster Rail/Road Bridge under construction prior to its opening in 1904. (City of Surrey Archives, 20.3.04)

NWSR was taken over by the Great Northern Railway. Access to New Westminster and Vancouver (circa 1900) was limited to the Brownsville Ferry and a barge car service by water from Liverpool to the Burrard Inlet for the next several years.

The bottleneck was relieved by the completion of the Fraser River Rail Bridge that lies adjacent to the present day Pattullo Bridge.

Elder statesman

Thomas Trapp sold his hardware store in 1929 and Thomas Dockrill Trapp (T. D.), the only surviving son, took over the Trapp Motors car franchise and moved the dealership to 891 Columbia Street.

Thomas Dockrill (T. D.) married Irene Belle Offer and they had three children: two sons, Thomas John and William George, and a daughter Nell Kathleen. T. D. was a city alderman in the 1930s and 1940s and following in his father's footsteps was president of the Royal Agriculture and Industrial Society whereby he had a chance to meet Winston Churchill.

Fig 11. Thomas Dockrill Trapp meets with Winston Churchill and New Westminster Mayor Wells Gray in Queens Park in 1929. (Photograph from the *Lougheed Mall Discover*, Spring 1991)

Of Thomas Dockrill's two sons, Thomas John (1913–2001) served overseas as sergeant from 1943 to 1945. When he returned from the War he took over the helm of Trapp Motors, until his retirement in 1974. He moved the business to North Road and Lougheed Highway in 1966–7. Thomas John was Past President of the local Canadian Club, Historian of the Hyak Anvil Battery, active member of Queen's Avenue Church, an avid yachtsman and honorary life member of the Royal Vancouver Yacht Club. Thomas John married Freda Field and the couple had three daughters, Karen, Susan and Mary.

William George (Bill) (1915–1982), T. D.'s other son, became a physician in Vancouver who specialized in thoracic surgery and was responsible for establishing the hyperbaric chamber at the Vancouver General Hospital. In the *Canadian Medical Journal and the Journal of Thoracic and Cardiovascular Surgery*, he described the use of the chamber in treating serious infection and as an intervention in intra-thoracic surgery. He played a leading role in the 5th International Hyperbaric Congress in 1973 and edited the proceedings of the meeting. Dr Bill Trapp died in 1982 but his contribution to medicine was recognised in 2004 by the opening of a new state-of-the-art hyperbaric chamber at the Vancouver General Hospital, thanks in part to a generous financial contribution from his family. The chamber complex named after him consists of three interconnected compartments and greatly enhances patient accessibility.

William George married Dorothy Murphy and had four children, Nancy, Paul, Lee and Gail. William George and his daughter Nancy were often invited by Ethlyn Trapp to travel with her to important events or on her European travels, as we shall see later.

In the years leading up to his death, in 1933, Thomas Trapp had become a respected "elder statesman" in the City of New Westminster. Trapp's involvement in the life and affairs of the City of New Westminster was extensive. He was president of the Westminster Trust and Secretary of the Board of Trade at its inception and President for three years. Trapp was one of a committee of three that established the city market at New Westminster. He was instrumental in starting Trapp Technical School and was New Westminster School Board chairman for twenty-one years.

Trapp Technical School was founded in 1920 in the old Provincial Gaol on Ontario Street, closing thirty-five years later. The jail was

Fig 12. T. J. Trapp, New Westminster Elder Statesman. (This photograph and extracts in the text are from F. W. Howay and E. O. S. Scholefield, "T. J. Trapp," *British Columbia Historical* [Vancouver: S. J. Clarke Publishing, 1914], 3:100–105.)

a macabre place to house a school; the solitary confinement cell in the basement was partially filled with earth, but generations of Tech students lifted the trap door to drop into the old cell for a quiet smoke.

Government records show that thirty-one men were hanged on the scaffold in the prison yard, often watched by crowds that gathered on the hill above the walls of the prison.[20] The first to hang was Tah-ak on January 6, 1863, and the last, Henry Jobes on December 5, 1911. Perhaps the most mysterious man in the jail was the Indian "Slumach," executed on January 16, 1891. Slumach was said to have come to New Westminster with his pockets filled with gold, dug from a secret horde in the mountains behind Pitt Lake. He would not reveal the location of his mine and, during his celebrations on Columbia Street, killed a man in a fight. As the story goes, his jailers begged him to reveal the mine's location, even as they placed the rope around his neck. This is one of numerous accounts of Slumach and his deeds in various "Legends of the Lost Creek Mine" and, like most legends, is inaccurate. Documents from the time indicate the truth was that Slumach was hanged for the killing of Louis Boulier, a half-French, half-Kanaka known as "Bee," near the Alouette River in Pitt Meadows. The stories of a lost mine are the material of legends.[21]

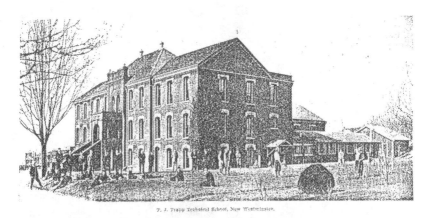

T. J. Trapp Technical School, New Westminster.

Fig 13. The provincial Jail in New Westminster, later the site of the Trapp Technical School. (Photograph from The British Columbian, May 21, 1955)

As an epilogue to the story of Thomas Trapp's brush with murder in the Nicola Valley, the same newspaper article recorded that Hare and the three brothers, Charlie, Archie and Allen McLean, were hanged in the same jail on Saturday, January 31, 1891.

In June 1986 the John Robson Elementary School, which occupied some of the buildings of the old Technical School, dedicated its library to T. J. Trapp in recognition of his contribution to the community.

Trapp's interest in youth was further demonstrated by his donating the land on which the Young Men's Christian Association building stood and by acting as President of the Association. Since his arrival in Canada, he had been an active member of the Presbyterian Church.

Thomas Trapp was President of the Royal Agricultural & Industrial Society of British Columbia for twenty years. When he retired as president, the organization gave him an embossed address and combination travelling bag along with glowing words of appreciation from which the following is taken:

Your business ability, integrity and zeal together with your public spirit and unselfish devotion to the best interests of the city have materially aided in its advancement and your constant advocacy and efforts to secure good roads, improved stock, better methods of land cultivation and good seeds have done much in the development of the agricultural life of this province.

A far cry from his first job ditch digging in Victoria.

In appreciation of his long service to the Royal City, Mayor Wells Gray presented him with a medal of good citizenship proffered by the Native Sons of British Columbia.[22]

Thomas Trapp died at home on January 19, 1933, at the age of ninety. His health had failed in the previous few weeks, though he had been well enough to visit his daughter Dorothy Countryman in St Paul, Minnesota, with his wife two months earlier. Following a service at St Andrew's Presbyterian Church he was laid to rest in the family grave in the Fraser Cemetery overlooking the Fraser River.

Nellie followed her husband just two years later.

Dr Ethlyn Trapp
"A life not chosen"

Childhood

Ethlyn Trapp, the daughter of a remarkable British Columbian pioneer, was born the fourth of eight children on July 18, 1891. A quiet Presbyterian upbringing led to a career in which she pioneered the medical specialty of Radiation Oncology in British Columbia and gained an international reputation, a life she later described as: *fortunate in so many ways, though not as I would have chosen.*

Her early life was in the home of a prosperous New Westminster family on Agnes Street overlooking the expanding city and the Fraser River. The house was in sight of the Brownsville Ferry carrying passengers and goods from the further bank of the river in South Westminster. The ferry, the only way to cross the river, was replaced when Ethlyn was thirteen by the railway bridge still in operation one hundred years later. Her father, Thomas, was forty-nine years old when Ethlyn was born. He had married Nellie Dockrill, sixteen years his junior, in 1886. Nellie's father, like her husband, was a pioneer Canadian who had come west to make a new life. The pair had eight children, four boys and four girls in the ten years from 1887 to 1897.

The children grew up in a strong Christian home and Ethlyn along with her brothers and two surviving sisters (the first born, Edith Kathleen, had died in infancy) would surely have followed their father and mother to Saint Andrew's Presbyterian Church a few blocks away on 7th Street twice or even three times on Sunday. Her father had the franchise for McLaughlin Carriages, so perhaps the children ran along beside their parents' carriage or, more likely, there may have been one for the children.

When Ethlyn was seven she witnessed firsthand the Great Fire of New Westminster. She must have feared for the loss of the family home just a block or two up the hill from the edge of the conflagration as it raced through the city along the waterfront. The children would have been raised from their beds by their parents in preparation for evacuation ahead of the fire. Fortunately the Trapp home was spared, but Ethlyn and her siblings must have spent a frightening night.

As well as their house in the city, the family kept a summer residence situated near the headwaters of Burrard Inlet, opposite Port Moody, where Nellie's father had first settled. The family called it "Sunnyside" and spent many summer holidays there. There were horses and a cow in the garden on Agnes Street, and Ethlyn, always adventurous, surely

Fig 14. The Trapp children in 1896. From the left on the back row, George, Thomas and Donovan. At the front Ethlyn, Neita and Stanley. (Photograph courtesy of Lynn Roseman)

learned to ride and perhaps compete with her brothers. She suffered a serious hip injury when tobogganing as a young girl that caused her to have a lifelong limp, but it never restricted her from taking on anything she had in mind.

Fig 15. The Trapp family photographed before the First World War. The three youngest boys standing to the left of their parents were pilots killed in the war. Ethlyn stands to the parents' right and next to her, Neita, who married a World War flying ace. (Photograph from the *Lougheed Mall Discover*, Spring 1991)

All Hallows School

Ethlyn attended public school in New Westminster and later All Hallows School for Girls in Yale, British Columbia.

In 1858, gold had been discovered on a gravel bar just 2 miles south of Yale on the Fraser River. The discovery caused a massive influx of people to pour into the region from all over the world, the majority of whom came from the California Gold Rush of 1849. Yale suddenly became a very large city with a population of 20,000 at the height of the gold rush and once was known as the biggest city west of Chicago and north of San Francisco.

In 1879, the Anglican Bishop, Acton Sillitoe, came to British Columbia from England. He became concerned with the welfare of native girls on reserves and also felt that there was a *"great need of higher education and culture"* in British Columbia. Bishop Sillitoe returned to England and visited All Hallows School in Ditchingham,

Fig 16. All Hallows School in Yale, British Columbia. "Brookside," the former home of railway contractor Andrew Onderdonk. (Courtesy of Yale Heritage Museum)

Norfolk.[23] He was impressed by the dedication of the Sisters who ran the school, as well as by the high standards of education provided. Upon his return to British Columbia, the bishop wrote to the Mother Superior of the English convent to ask if two or three of the Sisters from Ditchingham could come to British Columbia and establish a school for native girls. He was granted immediate consent, which exemplified the pioneering spirit and English influence that existed in the latter half of the nineteenth century.

When the Canadian Pacific Railway was completed in 1886, CPR Contractor Andrew Onderdonk donated "Brookside," his large home and property in Yale, to the sisters for use as a school, and All Hallows in the West was born, a unique establishment created with the best intentions of Anglican missionary zeal.

Bishop Sillitoe had also initiated the Columbian College for white girls in New Westminster in the early 1880s. This school collapsed due to lack of funds. Sillitoe proposed that the Sisters take in the girls from the college along with the native girls. They could use the money that had been promised to Columbian College by an English missionary

Fig 17. All Hallows School in Yale. Sisters and pupils relax. Although designed to allow native and white girls to integrate in their school life, no non-white faces are seen in this picture. (Image A-03609, courtesy of Royal BC Museum, BC Archives)

society. The Sisters agreed to Sillitoe's proposal, and plans for the establishment of a boarding school began. In 1890, All Hallows School was officially opened as a boarding school. It was the only school in Canada to admit both native and white girls in the same facilities. Thirty-five native girls and forty-five white girls were enrolled, ranging in age from six into the late teens. Many of the native girls were recruited by local Anglican clerics. When the school expanded to include the daughters of the white pioneers, a new addition was called the "Canadian School," and the old one, the "Indian School." The uniform of the girls in the "Canadian School" was a white dress with a violet sash in honour of Mrs Sillitoe.

Daughters of Anglican clergymen from across British Columbia were attracted to All Hallows. The clergy liked the school's religiously based instruction and thought it better to send them to a school in which their duty to God and man was taught from the highest of all motives. Another reason for attendance at All Hallows for some of the girls, both white and native, was the lack of educational alternatives elsewhere.

All Hallows became known for its overall high quality and standards of education so that the school flourished for twenty-five years. Nicolai Schou, a member of the school board in Manchester, England, was equally impressed when he visited All Hallows in the summer of 1890 to report on the school's examinations. He noted that the girls at All Hallows School had a good knowledge of the scriptures, and questions were as a rule well answered. He was also struck by the generally intelligent reading of the pupils, who in this respect compared favourably with most of the British Columbian boys of similar age he had heard. In 1907, one student of All Hallows placed first in British Columbia and sixth in Canada on the McGill University entrance exams. In 1908, another student received the first gold medal awarded in Canada by the Royal Academy of Music.

Although the original intention was that the native and white girls would be educated and live together, this did not last long. Almost certainly before Ethlyn attended the school, *"in accordance with the wishes of the English parents, the white children and the Indians [did] not mix,"* and in the early 1900s, *"Whites and Indians were never together. We weren't allowed to look at the Indian girls, not even in chapel which was the only time we ever saw them."* These quotes and a compelling and thorough review of the school are to be found in Jean Barman's *Indian and White Girls at All Hallows School.*[24]

Ethlyn's age when she first attended All Hallows is not recorded. She made friends with Daisy Dodd, daughter of William Dodd of Yale. There is a photograph of the students and teachers at the school taken in September 1899 in the archives of the Yale Historic Museum. The individuals in the picture are identified, including Daisy Dodd, but there is no mention of Ethlyn Trapp. Two girls are listed as being from New Westminster, and it is likely their families were known to the Trapps. In the school photograph Daisy would appear to be eleven or twelve years old, perhaps three or four years older than Ethlyn, who probably came to All Hallows about the age of ten to be joined by her younger sister Neita a year or two later.

Rail service from Vancouver to Yale began in the early 1880s and ran three times daily in order to carry supplies and workers for construction of the trans-Canada railway in the Fraser Canyon. The train run also made a popular excursion to Yale. When the railway was finished in 1885 the service was reduced, though a daily return schedule remained in effect until World War I. Ethlyn, and later her sister Neita, would almost certainly have been driven by her father in one of his McLaughlin carriages to board the train in Port Moody—the same route along North Road from Sapperton taken by her father some years earlier to court his future wife.

After the First World War, attendance at All Hallows dropped and funds were low. In 1920, the school was closed and the Sisters returned to England.

A reunion of former students, known as the "Old Girls," was held in Yale in 1966, attended by many of the alumni. There is no record of Ethlyn Trapp attending the reunion, but in her mid-seventies she might not have wanted to make the journey. The attendees donated a commemorative plaque, celebrating All Hallows in the West, that can still be viewed in the Church of St. John the Divine in Yale.

The Bugle Call

In the first few years of the twentieth century, the word "bugle" featured prominently in Ethlyn's young life. She must have been shown the photograph of her proud bearded father standing with the competitors in the "Laurie Bugle"(Fig 3). In addition, her eldest brother was a member of the famed bugle band of the New Westminster Companies of the 6th Regiment of the Duke of Connaught's Own Regiment (DCOR). The photograph of the band with teenaged T. D. proudly clutching his bugle (Fig 18) would have held a prominent place in 407 Agnes Street. In the days before telephones the bugle was used to spread information as rapidly as possible. During Ethlyn's coming of age, policing authorities were being formed, and existing army regiments were called upon not only to protect the peace but

Fig 18. Thomas (T. D.) Trapp stands third from the left in the front row of the famed Bugle Band of the New Westminster Companies of the 6th Regiment of the Duke of Connaught's Own Regiment. The photograph was probably taken about 1902 when T. D. would have been in his early teens. At least two of the members shown in the photograph died in the First World War. (City of Vancouver Archives, Mil P 146.)

also to protect early corporate interests of business against the union movement.

The Duke of Connaught, one of Queen Victoria's sons, became Canada's Governor-General in 1912. The Pipe and Bugle Band had been formed from his Regiment's original band in 1900. The Duke of Connaught's Own Regiment and the buglers played important roles in the history of British Columbia leading up to the First World War. The Steveston riots in July 1900 provided the Regiment with a call to arms as Aid to the Civil Power. At the time of the incident, Steveston was probably the world's largest salmon fishing centre. The white and native fishermen had gone on strike, whilst the Japanese fishermen decided to keep selling to the cannery. Though there had been no violence, the Reeve (elected head of a small municipality), with two justices of the peace, read the Riot Act to the strikers. When they did not disperse, he took the step of requesting military protection.

As only one in five homes had a telephone, buglers from the Regiment's Bugle Band rode around Vancouver calling assembly from trolley cars. Within a short time, four companies were assembled and were aboard the CPR Steamer Comox, bound for Steveston. Fortu-

Fig 19. On a 1914 ride to Yale, Ethlyn is with Donovan, Stanley and George each destined to be killed in The Great War. (Photograph courtesy of Lynn Roseman)

nately, the strikers dispersed, having received word of the army being on the way, and the Regiment disembarked to a quiet town.

In 1913 came another call to arms, this time for the Nanaimo Coal strike. When Chinese and Japanese strikebreakers were brought to the Nanaimo Coal Mines, one thousand striking miners went on the rampage. They took possession of the town, looting, burning, fighting and destroying property. Many innocent families, including women and children, took to the woods for their safety. The Premier, Sir Richard McBride, was away, but W. J. Bowser, Attorney General and Acting Premier, quickly called out the Militia. On the evening of May 13, 1913, a thousand men, including the 6th DCOR, sailed for Nanaimo. While the miners were holding a meeting in the Athletic Hall, the building was surrounded. A number of motorcars were so placed that their lights would play on the exits as the men came out. In groups of ten the strikers were marched between guards with fixed bayonets to the courthouse where the Riot Act was read and the strike was brought under control.

The Great War

Between 1909 and 1913, Ethlyn followed the usual route of the time for university education and attended McGill University.

In 1909 Ethlyn attended the McGill University College in Vancouver as a partial student. She studied English, French, German and History. The tuition cost for one session was ten dollars! The College began operations in 1906 in response to legislation enacted to establish higher education of both men and women in British Columbia. Ethlyn would have attended classes in vacant properties of the Vancouver City Hospital at the corner of Cambie and Pender Streets. The buildings were vacated when the hospital became the Vancouver General Hospital in 1905 and moved to its present location. In light of Ethlyn's later vocation in the radiation treatment of cancer, it is serendipitous that it was in the buildings of the City Hospital in 1902 that X-rays were first used in British Columbia. The McGill University College continued to offer classes until 1915 when the University of British Columbia was opened at its original Fairview location. In order to obtain a McGill University degree, the last year of classes had to be taken in Montreal.

For whatever reason, Ethlyn must have decided to take all three years of her degree course in Montreal, graduating with a BA in 1913. She only attended the College in Vancouver for one year. Living and studying in Montreal, Ethlyn would have stayed in the women's residence of the Royal Victoria College on Sherbrooke Street. Erected in 1899, thanks to Lord Strathcona's donation of £50,000, the building was a self-contained unit, serving as both dormitory and educational facility. Living in the Royal Victoria College meant belonging to a tight-knit community of women, particularly in the college's earliest years, when it was the centre of women's education at McGill. Music, athletics and academic societies flourished but were entirely separate from parallel activities undertaken by the university men.

According to the 1913 Old McGill Yearbook, Ethlyn was the vice-president of the Royal Victoria College. Her graduate write-up was as follows:

Miss Ethlyn Trapp. From New Westminster, B.C. Entered from "All Hallows," Yale B.C. Very much of a sport and the biggest tease in the year. Quote: "It ain't 'cause you bloomin' can't, it's 'cause you bloomin' won't."

Dr. Trapp's write-up in the 1927 Old McGill Yearbook further revealed her as a determined student:

Ethlyn Trapp. Quote: "Sing a song of stethoscopes, listening to their hearts; telling pleurisy from hives—fixing up their charts. When patients up and die, passing by the score—she just smiles and says—'Too bad, bring me in some more.'"

These comments from her time at McGill suggest an engaging personality that both then and in later years led to her election as president in a variety of professional and social spheres.

Ethlyn may have travelled to Montreal on the Canadian Pacific Railroad, probably in a Pullman car, where a black porter, recruited to work in Canada from the United States, would have attended her. Alternatively, one or more of her brothers may have driven with her in a family Buick. These were exciting times. In 1912, Ernest Rutherford, born in New Zealand, discovered the structure of the atom. He had been Chair of the Physics Department at McGill from 1898–1907 before he left to take the Chair at Manchester in England. McGill was a coeducational university but progress for women was abroad; McMaster University elected its first female student body representative. The Titanic hit an iceberg and sank in the Atlantic. Henry Ford instituted the assembly line in 1913, Fatty Arbuckle was one of the Keystone Kops and Houdini performed his magic.

The world changed a year later in August 1914. With declaration of war, patriotic support for Britain was profound across Canada. Had Ethlyn still been in Montreal, she might have joined the excited crowds in the city on the evening of August 3, 1914. The next day Britain would officially declare hostilities, ensuring Canada's official and all-but-obligatory entry into World War I. *"Separate French- and English-speaking crowds marched through their Montreal neighbourhoods, bellowing out 'La Marseillaise,' 'Rule Britannia' and 'God Save the King,'"* The next day, *"a cheerful mob invaded the Windsor Hotel in pursuit of the German consul."*[25]

In New Westminster, the Trapp family was equally willing to support the war half a world away. There were four boys in the family aged 19 to 26. The eldest, Thomas Dockrill Trapp (TD) reached the rank of Army Major in the First World War but was sent home because of malaria. The other three Trapp boys, Stanley (24), George (20) and Donovan (19) left to join the Royal Naval Air Service. Despite their patriotic desire to join the war effort and a wish to fly, it was not so easy to follow their chosen path. Although the actual path they took is unknown it may have been similar to that described by Raymond Collishaw in his book *Air Command: A Fighter Pilot's Story*.[26]

Collishaw was a Nanaimo boy who in an irony of fate, compared to the three Trapp boys, not only survived the war, but also became a highly decorated fighter pilot, rose to be Air Vice-Marshall and married Ethlyn's younger sister, Juaneita (Neita). Early in 1915 Collishaw (probably in much the same way as the three Trapp boys) had heard that the Royal Naval Air Service was recruiting pilots in Canada to join the war effort in Europe. Having previously attended a flying meet on Lulu Island, Raymond's interest in flying was already piqued. Consequently, he set out to apply, but joining up was easier said than done. He applied, was sent to Ottawa for interview, was accepted, but then told he had to find a private flying school, pay tuition and qualify for a certificate issued by the *Fédération Aéronautique Internationale*. Collishaw paid $400 to the only flying school in Canada, the Toronto Curtiss School, and waited, but it was nearly winter, and flying and training were being delayed. All that the many applicants wanted to do was to fly in the service of their country, but there was no help from politicians or government to make it possible. They applied to the Minister of Militia and Defence, whose reply to their spokesperson was:

My dear boy, you and your friends have indeed been led astray and I am sorry for you. I cannot see what possible use the aeroplane is in this war. If I were the commander of a force in the field and I wished to see what the enemy was doing I should climb a hill. If the hill was not high enough, then I should climb a tree on the hill. The aeroplane is an invention of the devil and all that it has done is to draw away from us many of our best young men. My advice to you and your friends is to forget all about it and join the infantry.

Unable to obtain the necessary training, Collishaw and seventeen of his colleagues were able to join a special company of the Royal Naval Canadian Volunteer Reserve aboard HMCS *Niobe* in Halifax harbour. Early in 1916 he was sent to Ottawa and then by rail to New York City to board the White Star liner *Adriatic*, destined for England. At the naval air station at Redcar, on the Yorkshire coast, he finally learned to fly. Although later described as one of Canada's finest flyers, his early reputation was as one of the most inept in landing the two-seater biplanes on which he was trained.

Not much information is available about the Trapp brothers war service, but it is known that all three died overseas—Stanley in 1916,

George in 1917 and Donovan in 1918. Three brothers killed in serving King and Country, one in each of three successive years. This was a numbing sacrifice for a single family from the far reaches of both an ocean and a continent.

There is some information known about George. When the war began he was a mechanical engineering student at McGill. Joining the Royal Naval Air Service (RNAS) in January 1917, he was posted in England to 10 Naval Squadron on July 2, 1917. He scored three victories flying the Sopwith Triplane, and three more flying the Sopwith Camel. He was killed in action by Bruno Justinius of Jasta 35 and buried at the Dozinghem Military Cemetery, Poperinge, West-Vlaanderen, in Belgium.

During the early stages of the war in France and Belgium, the aircraft of both sides were used only for reconnaissance and artillery observation. It was not until 1916 and later that advances in aircraft design and armament led to air fighting, carried out to allow continued observation behind enemy lines and to protect bombing raids into enemy territory. Collishaw and his many Canadian colleagues did most of their flying over and behind enemy lines.

Promoted to acting flight commander in July 1917, Collishaw led an early morning patrol that included George Trapp who had joined the squadron five days before. In the same month, Collishaw received the Distinguished Service Cross and was granted three months leave that enabled him to return home to Nanaimo. He broke his long rail journey across Canada to stop and visit the families of those he had known and flown with who had been killed in action. Among the families that he visited was that of George Trapp. He knew that George's brother Stanley had been killed in France on December 10, 1916. While visiting the family he met with the Trapp sisters, Neita and Dorothy, whom he described as "lovely girls, and I was immediately taken by one of them, Neita." The third sister, Ethlyn, would not have been at home since she was working in a military hospital during the war.

Following his visit to Nanaimo, Collishaw returned to New Westminster before he left for overseas, and there he and Neita became engaged. It proved to be a long engagement; it was nearly six years before they married, but as he explained, "getting married during the war seemed tantamount to asking a girl if she would like to become a young widow. Furthermore, I always believed that a young man should not marry too early; he should have a few years during which his adventurous spirit is not harnessed by the ties of matrimony." With his leave quickly over, he returned to Dunkirk and was posted to the Seaplane Defence Squadron at St. Pol. On his return to Europe, he learned of the death of George Trapp, which had occurred during his time in Canada.

During leave in 1923 from action in Iraq, Kurdistan and Russia, Raymond and Neita were finally married. Neita had travelled to England for the ceremony, accompanied by her sister Ethlyn who had interrupted her travels in the Far East to be with her sister.

Fig 20. Neita Trapp and Raymond Collishaw, photograph probably taken at the time of their engagement in the fall of 1917. (Photograph courtesy of the Vancouver Island Military Museum)

Balfour

Returning to British Columbia from McGill, Ethlyn attended a course in occupational therapy, but with the onset of the war she made her contribution to the war effort by volunteering in military hospitals in Vancouver and Revelstoke. It is not clear why, at the age of twenty-six, Ethlyn left Revelstoke to work in a sanatorium in Balfour on Kootenay Lake. Perhaps it was because she had heard of the place in an idyllic setting overlooking the lake or perhaps it was the start of her lifelong passion to travel, take on new challenges and explore new opportunities. It was a decision that probably changed her life. The sanatorium had been converted from a hotel that had been opened only a few years earlier and was magnificently situated just above the Ferry Landing in Balfour at the entrance to the west arm of Kootenay Lake. The hotel was one of the Canadian Pacific Railway hotels and had been built in the hope of attracting tourists to the southern reaches of British Columbia. Its remote setting and the onset of the First World War led to its demise and subsequent conversion to a sanatorium.

The building was three and a half stories in height. Two sides of the ground floor had a wide covered veranda previously open to the air, but now glassed in for protection from winter cold, without obscuring views of the lake. At one end a roofed but open tower had been created to enhance the enjoyment of the scenery. A large rotunda on the ground floor with an imposing stone fireplace, designed originally for fine occasions in the hotel, had been preserved. On the second floor many of the bedrooms were joined together into single wards with beds for twelve. At the rear of the building there was an annex for nursing staff, storage and recreational therapy.

If Ethlyn had travelled from Revelstoke, she would have sailed the Arrow Lakes and the Columbia River to Castlegar and then continued by train to Nelson, where she would have boarded one of the lake steamers for the twenty-mile trip to Balfour and then climbed the slope to the sanatorium. It is more likely that Ethlyn had returned home to New Westminster before taking up her position in Balfour.

The southern rail route from Vancouver to Nelson had been opened up by the creation of the Kettle Valley railway in 1916.

The prospect of the journey would have appealed to Ethlyn. As the train passed from Hope through the Coquihalla valley to Princeton, she would have been enchanted by the station names taken from Shakespeare— names such as Juliet, Romeo, Lear and Othello. From there the train made its way to Penticton, Midway, Castlegar and Nelson.

It was in Balfour that a young English patient was attracted to Ethlyn, and she to him. Transferred from the aftermath of war in Europe to recuperate from tuberculosis and the ravages of trench warfare, George Godwin was handsome, romantic and a married young father.

In a remarkable book[27] written several years later, about his life in the Great War, he tells of a young man's time in Balfour. Although not written in the first person it is almost certainly autobiographical and

Fig 21. A promotional tourist brochure, published by the Canadian Pacific Railway in about 1916 on the "Resorts in the Canadian Rockies," promoted some of the highlights that might be enjoyed by the traveller along the Crowsnest Pass Railway Route. (CPR Hotel, Balfour, c. 1917—1918, Nelson Museum Archives, 77.1.1 #174.)

supported by his known correspondence of future years. He described the reasons for his convalescence in British Columbia.

I went into hospital. They put me to bed and at night a volunteer nurse from the V.A.D turned me about. She did it expertly. She spoke of pleurisy. There was a chart above my cot. The man in the next cot said he had tuberculosis same as me. I did not have tuberculosis. Oh, dear, no. I was there because of the pain in my side. Pleurisy. And because of the damnable cough, and my voice that went back on me. I determined to ask the M.O. But when he came, I remained mute in the presence of this famous physician, for all the Army had made of me nothing but a captain. So it was the little V.A.D who told me the truth in the end but reproached me for she found it beastly to tell. She went away quickly. She was very young. I accepted the sentence with bitterness.

He tells how the pleurisy cleared up and he was allowed to get up. He was boarded and marked for transport to his home, but he had no wish to go. He could be in hospital, his pay would go on and he could assign the whole of his pay to his wife and two young children. He felt he had no ethical or financial choice other than returning home to England from hospital once his illness was under control.

A fortnight after the decision was made, he sailed out of Liverpool on a hospital ship bound for Portland, Maine. At Liverpool there had been no demonstration. The men merely embarked, and that was all. True, in each cabin there was a letter in the hand of King George, thanking them, wishing them Godspeed; but beyond that courtesy there was nothing, no public recognition of their effort and sacrifice. How different was the welcome in Portland. Men filed to the waiting train, or were carried to it. The train was white and very beautiful. Beside each cot there were gifts: books, fruit, chocolate, cigarettes, everything a man might care about with a journey to Vancouver ahead of him that would last six days.

It would be a year's paid recuperation at the hospital, they had told him, before he would be made right. He must go up into the mountains of British Columbia, to the Balfour Military Sanatorium on the hills by Kootenay Lake where the mountain air would cure him. The lung tissue would have time to heal. Then he would be as well as before.

Well, nearly as well: an arrested case.

In Balfour's isolated, idyllic setting, far from home, the therapists provided varied activity. The patients wove baskets and trays, which they gave as prizes to local youngsters. The grounds were sloped and cleared with wide paths on which people could pass at leisure. There were tennis courts for those who wished. Ethlyn, despite her childhood hip injury and limp, had played tennis at McGill and must have welcomed the opportunity to play again. Behind this grand building, the hills were partially treed and rose to the Kokanee Mountains and the Kokanee Glacier. In the summer there were pleasant strolls, which Ethlyn and George must surely have enjoyed, among the nearby orchards on the south facing slopes and, in the winter, walks in the brisk air and lightly snow-covered hills. It was difficult for Godwin to be nostalgic for Europe in these lovely surroundings and with the care offered by all around him. Of course he missed his wife and children but he knew at least they were financially provided for.

The friendship between the young couple would have been restrained by Ethlyn's strict Presbyterian family background—an upbringing and moral certitude that would not allow her to become involved with a married man, the father of two young children. George was at Balfour for nearly a year before he was returned to England, to home and family. It was twenty years later, just before the Second World War, that the pair met again and entered into correspondence, one side of which was retained by Ethlyn and will be referred to later in her life story.

With George's return to England, perhaps Ethlyn lost her enthusiasm for Balfour, and set out on travels to the Far East to put behind her this lost opportunity of love. Whether for this or for other reasons, she never married, even though she made many friendships throughout her life. Her travels in the first years of the 1920s took her to many parts of the world, including Singapore and the Dutch East Indies (Indonesia).

Fig 22. Ethlyn photographed in Vienna in 1929. (Dr Trapp's diary courtesy of Lynn Roseman)

Medicine Calls

One day, when in New Zealand, Ethlyn decided apparently quite suddenly that she would like to be a doctor. She promptly returned to Canada and enrolled in medical school at McGill in Montreal, graduating MD CM (Doctor of Medicine, Master of Surgery) in 1927. She interned in both the Montreal and Vancouver General Hospitals. Once more in keeping with her lifelong urge to travel and to seek further experience and training, she took a post as Assistant Surgeon in the Waipahu Hospital in Hawaii in 1929. Having gone west, she then turned east to undertake postgraduate work in General Medicine and Surgery in Vienna and Berlin before returning to New Westminster later in 1930.

Dr Trapp spent a year in general practice in New Westminster, concentrating on paediatrics where she made a lifelong friend

Fig 23. Dr Prowd who introduced Dr Trapp to radiotherapy. (Reproduced with permission of John E. Aldrich and Brian C. Lentle, eds., *A New Kind of Ray* [Vancouver: UBC Press, 1995])

of a children's doctor, Dr Reginald Kinsman. They both had schnauzer dogs, named Pooghie and Rudy respectively. General practice did not satisfy so Ethlyn travelled again into Europe to undertake postgraduate work in radiation therapy in Vienna, Stockholm and London for twelve months.

It is not clear why Dr Trapp should have turned to radiation therapy unless it was due to her contact with Dr Prowd, a radiologist with an interest in radiation treatment, in his private practice and at St Paul's Hospital. Returning from Europe, she joined Dr Prowd as an Assistant in Radiation Therapy at St Paul's Hospital in Vancouver, working there until 1935.

"A Pressing Medical Emergency"

Ethlyn Trapp played a leading role in establishing the first cancer clinic in British Columbia. The effort grew from a rising tide of opinion in the United Kingdom and Canada.

During the 1930s, across Europe, Central Canada and the Prairie Provinces, there was growing concern about the "cancer problem." British Columbia lagged behind. In response, the British Columbia Medical Association appointed a special committee to investigate the situation. Cooperation was sought from the Health Bureau of the Vancouver Board of Trade, and the Greater Vancouver Health League. On March 25, 1935, six men, two from each organization, met to consider the problem. They were Dr G. F. Strong and Dr H. H. Milburn of the BC Medical Association, Mr W. C. Ditmars and Mr W. J. Twiss, representing the Board of Trade; and Mr N. C. Levin and Dr B. J. Harrison from the Health League. They recommended a province-wide organization be formed "*to institute a concerted drive against this malady.*" The British Columbia Cancer Foundation was incorporated under the Societies' Act of the Province of British Columbia on May 21, 1935.

In order to garner more public support, the Board of Trade called a luncheon to be held in the Italian Room of the old Vancouver Hotel under the chairmanship of Mr T. S. Dixon, President of the Board of Trade. Invitations were sent to seventy-nine prominent lay and medical community leaders of whom thirty-nine attended on Wednesday June 12, 1935, at 12:30 PM. Dr G. F. Strong was asked to give a resumé of the present situation. He pointed out "*the great lack of facilities for the treatment of cancer—that British Columbia is the only province, Prince Edward Island excepted, which has no public supply of radium.*" He impressed upon the meeting the need for "*diagnosis and treatment; education of the medical men and the public; and clinical research. Technical details would be handled by a sub-committee of specialists, three of whom are Dr C. W. Prowd, Dr B. E. Harrison and Dr E. Trapp.*"[28]

Dr Trapp had been working with Dr Prowd for the previous three years at St Paul's Hospital, and Dr Harrison, the senior Radiologist at Vancouver General Hospital, had published a textbook on the subject. Almost certainly because of her appointment to the committee to study the technical aspects of radiation therapy needed for the establishment of a Cancer Clinic in Vancouver, Dr Trapp left on another of her world travels to study in various centres in Europe. In doing so, she wanted to make sure she knew that her opinions would be based on the most up-to-date information.

Prior to leaving for Europe, Dr Trapp spent three months in the Billings Hospital in Chicago.

During the next two years, she visited Brussels; Prof Chaoul in Berlin; Prof Holdfelder in Frankfurt; Prof Coutard and Prof Baclesse in Paris at the Curie Foundation; Prof Heyman and Prof Ahlom, in Stockholm at the Radiumhemmet; Dr Constance Wood in London; and Dr Ralston Paterson in Manchester. The last few months in Manchester, as Resident Medical Officer at the Holt Radium Institute, she later described as "*quite the most rewarding of the many I spent in post-graduate work.*"

At the aforementioned Board of Trade luncheon in June 1935, twenty-three people were nominated to form the executive committee of the British Columbia Cancer Foundation. Sixteen of these were not even present at the lunch! Dr Prowd spoke on the need for a Cancer Institute: "*This organized effort was going to meet a pressing medical emergency and statistics show that the death rate from cancer in British Columbia is the highest in Canada. To meet the cancer problem the Province should have an efficient Cancer Institute, and to provide this and carry out an effective educational programme will require at least $500,000.*"

Speaking on behalf of the Vancouver General Hospital, Dr A. K. Haywood said, "*In the General Hospital, the number of cancer patients was appalling. Modern equipment had been secured within recent years, and is now not adequate to keep pace with the number of cases being referred for treatment by the doctors.*" He went on to recommend, "*that a Cancer Institute be established in Vancouver, and offered to turn over to the Cancer Foundation a sum of money which he has in trust for a radium fund for the General Hospital.*" Just before the meeting adjourned at 2 PM, Mayor G. G. McGeer had the last word: "*a new era will open up, as soon as dividends are paid in human contentment, happiness and peace.*"[29]

The aims and objectives of the British Columbia Cancer Foundation (BCCF) set out at that time were the collection and distribution of funds and the improvement of diagnostic and treatment facilities for cancer patients throughout the province. These were to be achieved through the establishment of one fully equipped treatment centre with ancillary consultative and follow-up centres at various points across the province. The first officers elected were members of a formidable group: Honorary President, the Lieutenant-Governor, Mr J. W. Fordham Johnson; Honorary Vice President, Mr T. D. Pattullo, the Premier of the Province; and President Mr E. W. Hamber, who the same year followed Fordham Johnson as BC's Lieutenant-Governor.[30]

In the summer of 1936 the Board of Governors was enthusiastically searching for funds to establish the clinic. Letters were written to all the insurance companies in Vancouver seeking support in the following manner:

As you will see in the attached brief, the Foundation is affiliated with the British Empire Cancer Campaign and the main effort of the organization is to bring British Columbia into line with other Provinces in Canada in the provision of diagnostic facilities for early treatment. A great deal of preliminary work has been accomplished, and under enabling legislation of the British Columbia Government, the Foundation is now in possession of a substantial supply of radium which we are anxious to make available at the earliest possible moment by the provision of suitable accommodation and equipment.

The accompanying brief left no doubt as to the enthusiasm and expectation of those first Governors. It included:

Our objective is $600,000 for a provincial Cancer Institute of 50 beds, organized, equipped and managed to give prompt diagnosis and adequate treatment to cancer patients from all parts of the province and through constant and continued effort to provide funds by donation, grants and bequests for the maintenance of such Institute.

Our immediate proposal is for $150,000 to establish the first unit of 12 beds, permitting of provincial-wide organization of the cancer problem and providing for the diagnosis, needed treatment, the necessary follow-up and social services for cancer patients. This immediate proposal does not impair our ultimate objective and provides for immediate organization and treatment with the limited facilities at our disposal until the complete objective is realized."[31]

Dr Harrison and Dr Prowd made a strong appeal to the Vancouver Life Manager's Bureau for $100,000 to support the establishment of the Institute. The letter and brief, along with visits by various Governors, was sent to all insurance companies, including Canada, Confederation, Crown, Dominion, Great West Life, Imperial, London, Manufacturers, Mutual, North American, Sun and New York Life. Many expressed support but explained that they had already contributed to the cancer cause through their head offices back east! The effort did not produce anything but kind words.

A meeting of the Governors on December 1, 1936, resulted in a bill from the Hotel Vancouver for $41.40 that included $25 for twenty coffees, twenty canapés at 25 cents each, C.O.D. of $7.90 and $3.50 for cigars and cigarettes.

Early in 1936 the Directors of the Foundation had learned that 3.5

grams of unprocessed radium had come onto the market. On March 17, 1936, a committee under the chairmanship of Dr C. W. Prowd met the Premier, T. D. Pattullo, the Minister of Finance and the Provincial Secretary to request collaboration in the purchase of the radium at a price of $30,000 per gram. The price of radium had fallen from between $70,000–$100,000 per gram thanks to the discovery of radium in pitchblende ores near Great Bear Lake. On March 21 the Board of Governors of the BCCF passed the following resolution to comply with the terms of the BC Government Order-in-Council, guaranteeing the purchase of the radium:

Resolved that the Board of Governors purchase three and one-half grams of radium at a price not to exceed the sum of $105,000 and that the purchase be financed by the issue of a promissory note to the Dominion Bank in the sum of $105,000 or such lesser amount as may be required with interest thereon at the rate of 5% per annum as well as after as before maturity and that the Provincial Government be requested to guarantee the due payment of principal and interest on the said note or any renewals thereof. The radium to be insured against all risks. In consideration of the guarantee by the Province, the Board undertake to redeem the promissory note as early as practicable from the proceeds of the subscriptions, grants or bequests to the British Columbia Cancer Foundation and in any event within five years from the date hereof. The radium is to be kept within the Province of British Columbia and held by the British Columbia Cancer Foundation in trust for the Province until such time as the said promissory note and the interest thereon are discharged in full by the makers.[29]

The radium was purchased and arrived in Vancouver in May 1936. The total amount of radium was 3,533.14mgms and it was stored in the vaults of the Dominion Bank. The Bell-Irving Insurance Agencies Ltd insured the radium for $210.00 per annum.

The prevailing business conditions in November 1937 led to the postponement of a province-wide appeal for funds until the following year. However, a private appeal was considered to raise sufficient funds to process the available radium into needles and tubes suitable for clinical use. The members of the Foundation could not agree on what should be done with the radium. Frustration was expressed at the many differences of opinion and setbacks that had been encountered in the previous two and a half years.

The Board Minutes of December 30, 1937, included the following resolutions:

Whereas the B.C. Cancer Foundation was organized in May 1935 for the purpose of establishing a central institute for the control and treatment of cancer and whereas upon the strong representations from the Governors of this Foundation, the Government of the Province of British Columbia guaranteed the loan of $105,000 for the purchase of 3½ grams of radium and whereas the B.C. Cancer Foundation has not deemed it wise to proceed with a general public appeal for funds on a sufficient scale, either to carry out the original purpose of the Foundation or to repay the loan from the Government and in consequence the Foundation has no funds to continue the interest payments on the loan after December 31st: BE IT RESOLVED That the Government be so advised and BE IT FURTHER RESOLVED THAT THE B.C. Cancer Foundation shall not cease to work towards carrying out the original objectives of its Founders.

Further resolved: *"That a letter of appreciation and thanks be sent to His Honour the Lieutenant Governor (Mr E.W. Hamber) for his most generous help to the Foundation by the payment during the past year of interest on the loan for the purchase of radium."*

Progress a "Great Disappointment"

The Committee on the Study of Cancer of the British Columbia Medical Association, now including Dr Trapp who had recently returned from her fact-finding visits in Europe, was supportive of the Foundation from the outset and especially in 1937, 1938, and 1939 and the early war years. Dr Trapp was chairman of the BCMA committee in 1941.

Under president Dr A. Y. McNair and secretary Dr Ethlyn Trapp, the following resolution was approved on November 22, 1937, and forwarded to the Foundation:

WHEREAS the Committee on the Study of Cancer of the British Columbia Medical Association in 1935 brought to the attention of certain lay groups the urgency of the cancer situation in B.C. and recommended that a provincial wide organization be formed to undertake the raising of the necessary funds to establish a Cancer Foundation for British Columbia

AND WHEREAS to date our facilities for treating Cancer are grossly inadequate and the urgency for better means of Cancer treatment is being more and more apparent as time goes on

BE IT RESOLVED THAT the Committee respectfully urge that a provincial wide campaign to raise funds be undertaken with the least amount of delay.[32]

Five months later the Committee expressed its frustration at the lack of progress:

Some three years ago the Cancer Committee of this Association initiated a movement which resulted in the formation of the BC Cancer Foundation, whose main objective was the unification of activities in the field of Cancer Control in British Columbia under the one organization. This included the establishment of a central Cancer Institute and subsidiary Cancer Centres elsewhere in the Province as the plan developed. The plan was in accord with the recognized better ones in effect in some European countries, notably Sweden, where cancer treatment is admittedly more advanced than it is on this continent. Unfortunately the progress made by the BC Cancer Foundation has been a great disappointment, and we find our problem about as it was three years ago.

Dr Ethlyn Trapp, along with Drs B. J. Harrison and C. W. Prowd, was appointed to work with three members of the Foundation to supervise the use of the irradiation facilities supplied to the Cancer Foundation. The medical directors of the Foundation at that time (Drs Milburn, Thomson, Trapp and Harrison) were opposed to the radium being processed and made available to hospitals around the province as had been suggested. The Minister of Finance for British Columbia responded to the Board's resolution of December 1937 on April 13, 1938, that the Government expected the Foundation to meet its obligations with regard to radium. Faced with this demand, the Directors agreed to establish a campaign for funds, in cooperation with the Cancer Division of the BC Medical Association and the Canadian Medical Association Department of Cancer Control, to discharge their obligations.

In 1938 a bequest of $50,000 from an anonymous benefactress (whose name has never been publicly released), however, provided the catalyst to create the Institute. The bequest included a number of conditions.[33] The money was to be spent in four ways: $30,000 for one gram of the radium held in the Dominion Bank, $10,000 for processing it, $9,000 for purchasing and equipping the house on Thirteenth Avenue granted by the Vancouver General Hospital and $1,000 for alteration necessary to convert it into a suitable unit.

Fig 24. The plaque of the anonymous bequest that allowed the British Columbia Cancer Institute to be established. (BC Cancer Agency, Multimedia Services)

The bequest gave direction for these expenditures to be under the direction of Dr J. W. Thomson and Dr B. J. Harrison. It also indicated that the unit be under a Director and Assistant Director who would be honorary, that surgeons could use the radium provided it was *"under the direction and at the discretion of the Radiologist."* In recognition of this seminal donation a plaque was placed at the entry to the Clinic. The wording caused some concern, but with the aid of the Chairman of the Department of English at the University of British Columbia (UBC), a suitable inscription was penned, including a quotation from 1st Corinthians, Chapter 3, verse 13: *"Every Man's Work Shall be made Manifest."*

In accordance with the terms of the bequest, $30,189.95 worth of the radium was sent to New York in May 1938 and then to Belgium to be processed into 188 needles and 82 tubes of various strengths. The radium content of the needles and tubes was verified in Ottawa on their return journey to Vancouver. The first home for the treatment centre was made possible by Vancouver General Hospital's offer to make available the former intern's residence at the corner of Heather Street and 11th Avenue and to supply heat, lighting and nursing services. Alterations to the building, including carpentry, plumbing, electrical work, an oil burner and linoleum on all floors, were estimated at $2,914. The building on 13th Avenue mentioned in the bequest was not thought to be suitable.

And so the opening of the clinic that Dr Trapp and so many others had worked so hard and long to create was about to be realized. In preparation for the opening, a Radium Therapist and two part-time medical men were appointed. The honorary Secretary, G. M. Shrum, appointed Dr Maxwell Evans by letter on October 17, 1938: *"Upon the recommendation of Dr B. J. Harrison [the honorary director of the clinic] you were appointed the full-time Radium Therapist for the Institute on the following basis. Salary $100.00 for the period October 1, 1938 to November 1, 1938 and $4,000.00 per year thereafter."*

The BC Cancer Institute Opens

The British Columbia Cancer Institute clinic opened on Saturday November 5, 1938. The occasion was recorded the same day in the *Vancouver Sun* in rather flowery prose under a full-page headline: "*Precious Radium Needles Arrive; Cancer Clinic to Begin Work on Monday, Ceremonies Today Mark Realization of Dreams, Clinic Staff Takes Extraordinary Precautions for Handling of Curative, but Deadly Element.*"

The story continued:

Ten tiny needles, each less than an inch long—gramophone needles they look like. Ten passports to surcease from human suffering to freedom from the great scourge of mankind—cancer. They lay on a leaden shield in the unfitted laboratory.

Fig 25. The entrance to the first BC Cancer Institute on the corner of Heather Street and Eleventh Avenue across from the Vancouver General Hospital. (BC Cancer Agency, Multimedia Services)

This afternoon, at three o'clock, Hon. Eric W. Hamber, lieutenant governor of British Columbia, formally opened the clinic, and Hon. G. M. Weir, minister of health unveiled a plaque honouring "the unknown" donor of $50,000 which permitted the early opening of the clinic.

But the "Day" so far as the staff is concerned was Friday, when the 270 needles came back from a long trip to Belgium. The radium came into the building quite casually, in the arms of Dr G. M. Shrum, honorary secretary of the BC Cancer Foundation. There were eight small wooden boxes, wrapped in brown paper and carefully sealed. Dr Shrum dumped the boxes on a laboratory bench, seized a screwdriver and pried a box open. Within were innumerable wrappings of paper, and in their midst—multum in parvo—a small round lead box. And within this with more wrappings, the ten needles, first of the 270 to see the light in their permanent home.

Four days later the first patient was treated. So began the story of the British Columbia Cancer Institute (BCCI) under the responsibility of the BC Cancer Foundation, conceived and brought to life in large measure by the efforts of Ethlyn Trapp. The Institute struggled through the war and had its ups and downs thereafter until falling under the responsibility of the Provincial Government as the Cancer Control Agency of British Columbia in 1974.

Ethlyn Trapp returned to her private practice in downtown Vancouver, only to be called back to the Institute in 1940 when Dr Evans, now the Medical Superintendent, left for war service.

The early war years provided considerable financial hardship to the Institute. In the summer of 1940, in an effort to raise funds, a grand Symphony Concert was arranged for Saturday, August 17.

The concert was held in the Malkin Bowl in Stanley Park at 8.30 PM. W. H. Malkin was the incumbent president of the BC Cancer Foundation. The Park Board donated the use of the Bowl and 4,000 chairs. There were 500 tickets available at $2 each, 500 at $1.50, 200 at $1.00 and 1000 at 50 cents. In the unlikely event of rain, the concert was to be held in the Forum at a rent of $250. Nevertheless $400 rain insurance was taken at $10.48 per hundred. The Provincial Government cancelled the amusement tax on the concert! The Vancouver

Symphony Orchestra and Mr Jan Cherniavsky, pianist, donated their services. The Kitsilano Boy's Band assisted the Orchestra and received $25 to cover expenses. Mr John Brownlee, the noted baritone of the Metropolitan Opera, received $500 and return airfare to Hollywood. The following Monday the *Vancouver Daily Province* reported a large and appreciative audience, and described the gifted Australian Brownlee's performance as a gratifying success, but the Foundation's records do not report the financial outcome.

A Wartime Institute

In the late summer of 1940, Dr Evans left for military service overseas, whereupon Dr Ethlyn Trapp was appointed Acting Medical Superintendent at a salary of $233.33 per month.

In 1940 the cost of operating the Institute was listed as about $825 per month with revenue from all sources of about $400! The minutes of the Executive Committee of the BCCI in 1940 record that 317 patients were registered in the year and that monthly expenditures totalled $9,153.77 for the year. This included salaries of $7,253.07, wages of $720, telephone expenses of $141.70, insurance of $294 and estimated office and clinical expenses of $365 and $380 respectively. The Board of Management of the Institute, in facing these financial woes, recommended the following plan:

a) *Arrangements be made to receive new patients on Tuesdays and Fridays only.*

b) *That the services of the part time nurse be dispensed with and a consequent extension of the work of the full time nurse and secretary be arranged.*

c) *That the services of the assistant radiologist be dispensed with and that a part time medical intern be engaged. In this connection it is understood that a possible arrangement might be arrived at whereby the part time medical intern would be lodged and fed by the Vancouver General Hospital and spend half time at work on the wards of the Vancouver General Hospital.*[33]

It was predicted that these modifications would result in a saving of $100–125 per month, but that within a year, further funds would have to be found to carry on. The Board of the BC Cancer Foundation accepted the recommendations but went further and suggested that each Governor of the Foundation contribute $20 per annum to the operating expenses of the Institute for the duration of the war and that the Provincial Government be asked to make up the emergency deficit of $5,000 per year.

In September 1940 the British Columbia Medical Association (BCMA) recommended, *"that the activities of the British Columbia Cancer Institute be limited to treatment of malignant conditions."* Dr Trapp, who was also a member of the Board of the BCMA, immediately encouraged the Board to change its view and accept that *"certain non-malignant cases should be treated by radium at the Institute."*[34]

Ever aware of the dangers of war, Dr Trapp reported in May 1942, *"For Air Raid precautions the radium safe and the radium is now stored in the basement fireplace."*[35]

On March 19 the chairman of the Foundation, Mr W. H. Malkin and Dr Trapp met with representatives of Victor X-ray Corporation and the Ferranti X-ray Company to receive quotations. Dr Trapp, Dr Harrison and Dr G. M. Shrum, Head of the Department of Physics, University of British Columbia, recommended the purchase of a Maximar "250" Therapy X-ray unit, manufactured by the Victor X-ray Corporation, for $8,825.00, with various cones, a hydraulic couch, physics equipment and structural modifications to a total of $14,593.75. This recommendation was accepted by the Board of the Foundation on March 30 and presumably forwarded to the Government the following day. However, the recommended X-ray machine was not purchased.

Dr Trapp asked Dr Margaret Hardie to join her at the Institute on a part-time basis on September 4, 1942. Margaret (Mardi) Hardie grew up in Victoria where she received her early education. She obtained a Teacher's Certificate and taught school in Victoria for several years. Dr Hardie graduated from the University of Toronto in 1924 with an M.B. and earned her Big "T" as the champion women's tennis player. Due to health reasons and raising a young family, she did not return to medicine until 1942, when asked by Dr Trapp to come and help out at the Institute. Dr Hardie undertook some intern duties at the Vancouver General hospital while working at the Cancer Institute and passed her LMCC (Licentiate of the Medical Council of Canada) in 1944. This was quite an accomplishment considering the years since graduation, working and running a busy household with two teenaged daughters and a seven-year-old boy.

Dr Hardie took a special interest in gynaecological cancer. In the early 1950s she studied in Manchester, England, and Upsala, Sweden. She successfully wrote her specialist examination in therapeutic radiology in 1953 at the age of 55. She ran the gynaecological service at the BCCI until her retirement on December 31, 1961. On retirement, she and her husband Rod travelled around the world on a freighter. At the Club Med in Agadir, Morocco, they became bridge champions of North Africa, even though the language was French of which they knew little.

Financial difficulties at the Institute persisted and in February 1943, the Premier of the Province, John Hart, agreed to a grant of $4,000 to the Institute for the remainder of the fiscal year. A grant for the following year was not forthcoming and the Premier suggested, "*the Institute should try to carry on with its own resources.*"[36]

Dr Trapp's title was changed to Medical Director in September 1943. With no further progress in acquiring X-ray equipment, in March of the following spring, Dr Trapp offered to transfer her own equipment from her private office to the Institute. If Dr Trapp were to have done this, she would have had to give up her private practice. The fact that the Institute had no X-ray equipment severely limited its ability to provide a service to cancer patients. The Institute had radium, but so did several others in the province, including St Paul's, the Vancouver General Hospital and Dr Trapp and Dr Sadler in their private practices. It was suggested that if she did transfer her own equipment, she should be appointed full-time Medical Director for the duration of the war or until Dr Evans's return. Why did the BC Cancer Foundation which was responsible for the Institute, not accept Dr Trapp's offer to limit her time as Director, after which she would have had to re-establish her private practice? Was this a result of the male-dominated Foundation being reluctant to appoint a woman? Dr Trapp already enjoyed the favour of the support of the BCMA as one of its directors and was well known beyond the boundaries of the province. Or was it a sense of obligation to Dr Evans who had held the title of Medical Superintendent at the time he left for military service overseas?

Before completing any arrangement with Dr Trapp, the Foundation made a further approach to government in July including the following submission:

Had the war not intervened it is possible that a complete cancer service might have grown from the original Institute in the course of a few years. Nevertheless, in spite of our limitations we have been able to provide, since our opening, diagnostic and treatment facilities for some 2000 patients from all parts of the Province. We have given 1,986 radium treatments and referred 600 patients for x-ray therapy. We have been advised by our Honorary Attending Staff that it will be necessary to provide certain extra facilities. We are, therefore, asking the Provincial Government to purchase an x-ray equipment which can be immediately installed in the present Institute. This machine would be the property of the Provincial Government, placed on loan to the Institute."

The same report of 1944 included the first indication of the eventual establishment of the British Columbia Cancer Agency. "It is our hope that the Government of British Columbia may eventually undertake the control of cancer as has been done in the case of tuberculosis and venereal disease. If and when such a scheme is initiated, the Cancer Foundation is prepared to withdraw from the active treatment of cancer, to cooperate with the Government as an auxiliary or in any other way and to continue to use our endowments and income in the interests of cancer through education and research."[37]

Return to Private Practice

W hen Dr Evans came home from the war, Dr Trapp handed back to him a rapidly growing Institute and went off to New York for a refresher course. She visited Dr F. W. Stewart at Memorial Hospital, New York, and Dr Papanicolaou at the New York Hospital to "work in cancer histology" for three months and then returned to her own private practice in Vancouver. She was in partnership with Dr Olive Sadler at 925 West Georgia Street from 1946 until 1960.

In one of her many lectures Dr Trapp spoke in Chilliwack in March 1953 on the birth of cancer services in Canada:

It was the Canadian Medical Association which initiated organized plans for cancer control in Canada. This was about ten years after the British Empire Cancer Campaign had been founded in Great Britain. The CMA formed its first Cancer Committee in 1933. Subsequently, Cancer Committees were formed in each province—but these were not too active. Then came the King George V Silver Jubilee Cancer Campaign. This was not a phenomenal success financially but it stimulated the interest of the whole country in cancer.

Although very interested in cancer education and research, she said, *"in this consuming desire to discover the cause of cancer we must not lose sight of our immediate problem— the cancer patient, the man or woman or child who has cancer; for as the Chinese say, 'it is better to save one man's life than to build a seven story pagoda.'"*[38]

In December 1956, when she wrote on the establishment of a cancer centre in Costa Rica, her remarks were prophetic and applicable today:

My own opinion is that there should be initial centralization as recommended in our report of 1951 with a plan for the development of a certain amount of decentralization in the years to come, after a central institute has become well established. By decentralization I mean the later setting-up of some subsidiary treatment and diagnostic services but always in co-operation with the central institute. This would presuppose an overall plan with integration of records, etc.[39]

Despite her advocacy for centralized cancer care, both in her support for the establishment of the BC Cancer Institute and in lectures and writings, Dr Trapp remained in private practice for the rest of her career. In a letter of reply to an aspiring applicant for a post in British Columbia, she wrote, *"Private radiotherapy is a lost cause in this province because radiotherapy is subsidized under hospital insurance for those patients who are in hospital. This will soon be the case right across Canada."* Of course, the advent of Cobalt therapy, which could not be housed in a medical office building, must surely have severely damaged the prospects for private radiotherapy in Canada.

Dr Trapp and Dr Olive Sadler were in practice together in the Medical Building on Georgia Street. Dr Sadler was born in Ottawa in 1898 but grew up in Victoria. She obtained a BA from the University of British Columbia in 1919 and a masters degree in bacteriology and chemistry in 1921. She was married and widowed at an early age and turned to medicine in the late 1930s. Dr Sadler qualified from McGill in 1940 and interned in San Francisco. She received certification in therapeutic radiology in 1949 following training in various centres in the United States. In addition to her career as a physician, she had wide ranging interests, many of them similar to those of her partnership colleague. She was active in the Canadian Federation of Medical Women, the Red Cross, St. John Ambulance, the British Medical Association, the Anglican Church, the Vancouver Art Gallery and the Society for the Prevention of Cruelty to Animals. Dr Sadler died in September 1975 at the age of 77. Dr Trapp and Dr Sadler held hospital privileges at the Royal Columbian Hospital in New Westminster from 1954. On occasion they were also called upon to treat patients in other Lower Mainland hospitals. They would transport radium in the trunks of their cars en route to the required hospital. Ethlyn had a passion for convertible cars, usually supplied by the family business at Trapp Motors. A particular favourite was a yellow roadster.

On Ethlyn's death, Olive Sadler wrote in her "appreciation": *"In order to be able to treat her patients without the limits imposed by the existing bureaucracy she used her private fortune to establish a modern and very well equipped treatment centre."*[40]

The first equipment in the office shared by Drs Trapp and Sadler was the Siemen's Stabilivolt 200KV orthovoltage treatment machine that could also operate at 120–135KV for treatment of skin and superficial diseases. Around 1951 Dr Trapp purchased the General Electric Maximar 240KV machine for their office in Vancouver.

The practice of radiation oncology, or radiotherapy as it was known in the middle years of the last century, was very different to that of later years and the present day. Equipment was limited to orthovoltage X-rays and radium. The limited energy of the X-rays meant that they could be used in private offices with only minor additional protection required for the caregivers and patients. Similarly, radium could be handled with care and applied to the patient's skin for minutes or an hour or two in the physician's office. If radium was used internally—for example, in the treatment of gynaecological cancer— this was done under hospital care. Drs Trapp and Sadler carried out these treatments in the Royal Columbian Hospital in New Westminster and the Vancouver General, St Paul's and St Vincent's Hospitals in Vancouver. The majority of treatments given using X-rays were for benign conditions, in stark contrast to modern day radiation practice.

Dr Trapp's records of treatment are housed in alphabetical order in the storerooms of the BC Cancer Agency. A review of the first 100 records beginning with the letter "A," showed that three-quarters of the patients were treated for benign conditions. Eleven were infants who received X-rays for thymic enlargement, a practice abandoned in the early 1950s, and fifteen infants or children received radium or X-ray treatment for birthmarks (haemangiomata). Most of these children were followed by their family physician and not seen again by the treating radiation physician and thus the outcome of the treatment is not recorded. The symptoms arising from tonsillar or adenoidal enlargement were treated in thirteen people. Benign skin disease was treated in ten, plantar warts in six, arthritis in four, menorrhagia in seven and other benign conditions in ten patients. With very few exceptions, none of these patients would have been offered X-rays or radium in modern radiation oncology practice. Twenty-four patients were treated for malignant disease, four postmastectomy for breast cancer and seven for palliation of symptoms from various malignancies. Four basal cell carcinomas were treated with radium application or X-rays, not dissimilar to that which might be used today. Nine patients were treated for carcinomas of the cervix or uterus with a combination of X-rays and radium similar to today's practice, the X-ray treatment given daily over several weeks and the radium or caesium in one or two applications a week apart. The radiotherapy records do not contain follow-up information and in many cases are not signed, preventing attribution to either Dr Trapp or Dr Sadler.

The acquisition of a Cobalt Megavoltage treatment machine by the BC Cancer Institute in 1952 ushered in the demise of private treatment clinics and treatment in individual hospitals such as St Paul's and the Vancouver General Hospital. Megavoltage treatment, later including linear accelerators, was more efficient in reaching deep-seated tumours and created fewer side effects. However, the medical community in British Columbia was slow to appreciate the advantages, and Dr Trapp and others, especially at St Paul's Hospital, continued to use ortho-voltage therapy alone until retirement or closure of radiation treatment departments at the turn of the decade and into the mid 1960s. Drs Trapp and Sadler also had radium for gynaecological cancer and for implant of skin and lip cancers. This author has not been able to find where and when Dr Trapp purchased radium sources except for the acquisition of Heyman's capsules from Stockholm. In December 1947 she ordered Heyman applicators for the treatment of cancer of the uterus from the Karolinska Institut in Stockholm for her practice, at a cost of 240 Swedish Croner. They were delivered in February by the Railway Express Agency at a cost of $3.01

A Prophet in her Own Land

Dr Trapp was elected president of the British Columbia Medical Association (1946–1947) and president of the National Cancer Institute of Canada (1952), being the first woman to hold either of these posts.

Dr Trapp assumed the presidency of the BCMA at its annual meeting on June 11, 1946, held in Alberta at the Banff Springs Hotel. Her year in office was relatively quiet, though the issues were often not too different from those of the present day. In the January 1947 meeting it was minuted that *"consideration should be given to the acute lack of sufficient hospital accommodation in Vancouver. The present conditions were aggravated by the difficulty in securing adequate nursing service."*

Fig.26. Dr Ethlyn Trapp, the first female president of the British Columbia Medical Association and the first female president of the National Cancer Institute of Canada. (Archives of the BC Medical Association)

As president of the BCMA, Dr Trapp was involved in discussions regarding the formation of a medical school at the University of British Columbia. She had written to Dr R. R. Struthers, Assistant Director of Medical Sciences at the Rockefeller Foundation in New York, to solicit his views. Although he agreed that the university should have a medical school, he expressed various reservations, such as: "*But certainly not one of an inferior character.*" He reported how he "*discussed the possible budget with Dr Desbrisay some three years ago and was even then amazed at the inadequate salaries that were proposed.*" He went on to write: "*as you know, I am moderately conversant with the various political forces at play in the medical world in Vancouver, and I would think it essential for the success of the school that any Dean being hired should be given if possible a fairly free hand away from the politics of the Vancouver General Hospital.*"

Following further correspondence between the two, Struthers wrote to Trapp: "*I am distressed for you, though not surprised, that the establishment of your University Medical School is causing so much heartache.*" He concluded his letter addressed to Dr Trapp at her office in the Medical Dental Building in Vancouver: "*I noticed that your note is signed 'As always, in haste' I am still looking forward to the day when you are not sitting in an airplane, or so rushed with your practice and your presidency of the British Columbia Medical that you can really sit down and tell me some of the things you are reading, thinking and doing.*"

Dr Gordon Richards, the "father" of radiotherapy in Toronto, proposed her for the Board of Directors of the National Cancer Institute of Canada and when she became president of the NCIC, she had control of an annual budget of $470,000 but pledged to continue her private practice of radiotherapy.

Dr Trapp gave the Osler Lecture to the Vancouver Medical Society at the Hotel Vancouver on March 4, 1952—she was the first woman to be invited to give the lecture, choosing as her topic "Modern Alchemy." In her talk she traced the development of electricity in its relation to matter and its later application to nuclear fission and medical science. Following her lecture she received many letters of congratulation, one from "William," in the Department of Pathology at the University of British Columbia (UBC), included the following: *"May I add that the charm of the speaker and the little flashes of femininity made the grave matter of the discourse so acceptable and indeed entrancing."*

In January 1952 the Honorary Secretary of the Royal College of Physicians & Surgeons of Canada wrote Dr Trapp to thank her for service on the Specialty Committee in Radiology. The letter included the phrase *"the College has indeed been fortunate to have had as members of the specialty committees men like yourself."* Ethlyn underlined the word men in red and added an exclamation mark, but did not reply!

Dr Trapp's honours included the degree of Doctor of Science from UBC in 1954 in recognition of her contribution to medicine in British Columbia and the country. In her letter of appreciation she wrote: *"In addition to my delight at being given the honour, I have the added pleasure of receiving it when the first class in medicine receive their degrees and when Dr Brock Chisholm gives the graduation address."*

The citation on presentation at the ceremony read:

Mr. Chancellor, long ago the Roman writer Ovid, abandoning his habitual flippancy, used the phrase malum immedicabile cancer— "cancer, an incurable evil." To day we have with us a medical scientist and a gifted woman who has spent her utmost efforts to take from the description of this disease the word incurable.

Dr. Ethlyn Trapp was born in New Westminster, the daughter of a well-known and well-respected pioneer family. After graduating from the Medical School of McGill University, she did post-graduate work in radiation-therapy in Paris, Stockholm, Manchester, and London, and is now one of the leading radiologists of the North American continent.

In 1946 she was the first woman to be elected President of the B.C. Medical Association, and in 1952 was the first woman to give the Osler Lecture. In this latter year she was also elected President of the National Cancer Institute of Canada.

She is one of those who has been instrumental in developing modern cancer-treatment throughout this country and this continent, and has been inspiringly and consistently unselfish in giving skill and effort and support in combating a terrible ravager of mankind.

In recognition of her achievements and of the generous and unselfish devotion from which they arose, I now present to you, Sir, for the degree of Doctor of Science, honoris causa, Dr. Ethlyn Trapp.

At the request of Harold Johns, Canada's pre-eminent radiation physicist of the time, Dr Trapp was asked to be the Western Provinces representative on a committee for *"Post-graduate training of radiation physicists in Canada."* She was also a member of the Advisory Committee on Radiation Therapy involved with revision of the Minimum Standards for Radiation Therapy Centres in 1954.

Fig 27. Ethlyn Trapp receives the Order of Canada from the Governor General, The Rt Hon Roland Michener in 1968. (Photograph courtesy of the British Columbia Medical Association)

Dr Trapp was awarded Fellowship without examination in the charter year of the Faculty of Radiologists in 1954.The letter offering the Fellowship from the President, Peter Kerley, at Lincoln's Inn Fields in London, on April 7, 1954, read:

The Council of the Faculty of Radiologists was empowered in its Royal Charter to award a limited number of Fellowships without examination in the Charter year to members who have distinguished themselves in their specialty. It gives us great pleasure to inform you that you have been awarded the Fellowship by the Council in this Charter year. This will be formally conveyed to you in absentia during the Ceremony of Admission to be held in London on Friday May 1st. The fee payable before admission is 20 guineas.

In accepting the privilege, Dr Trapp duly forwarded her 20 guineas in fees!

In 1954 Dr Trapp was elected to Honorary Membership of the Medical Women's International Association. In March the following year she took part in a panel discussion on Cancer of the Cervix at the UBC Refresher Course in Obstetrics and Gynaecology.

Simeon Cantrill of the Swedish Hospital in Seattle wrote to Trapp and others in 1957 wanting to promote a study of cancer of the cervix based on the work of Ruth Graham in Boston. Trapp welcomed the initiative, but regretted that she and Dr Sadler had only a small number of such patients, perhaps 100 in the last six years.

In 1963 she received a citation by the Canadian Medical Association for her work in cancer research and in 1968 a medal of service of the Order of Canada.

When Ethlyn received the Order of Canada, she was allowed one guest and she took her physician nephew W. G. Trapp. Ethlyn was notorious for always being late, causing W. G. to pace the hotel lobby in anxious anticipation of missing the ceremony. Ethlyn finally arrived and reassured him that there would be no difficulty. As they left the hotel, the federal Finance Minister of the time was about to get into his impressive limousine when Ethlyn interjected and asked if he was going her way. He was and agreed to Ethlyn's request for a lift. She and her anxious guest arrived in style!

International Recognition and Friendships

Dr Trapp was respected by her peers and admired by the many friends she made on her travels and in her work. Her love of travel was indeed prodigious. Following her young adult journeys after the First World War to Singapore, Indonesia and New Zealand, there were her postgraduate study visits to Vienna, Berlin, Stockholm, London, Brussels, Frankfurt, Paris, Manchester, Chicago and New York. She travelled to meetings around the world and took the opportunity to visit Warsaw, Athens, Istanbul, Rome, Havana, Bermuda, South America and China as well as the major cities in Canada and in the Eastern and Western States of America. In many of these places she made friends and corresponded frequently, returning their friendship and hospitality whenever they visited in Vancouver. She was particularly helpful to friends she had made in Europe before the War, both in Germany and Great Britain. Throughout the 1940s and '50s she received numerous requests from around the world for advice and information, many of which she forwarded to Dr Evans or the National Cancer Institute of Canada (NCIC) for their response. Many of Europe's leading radiotherapists of the time were frequent correspondents. In a letter to Ralston Paterson, one of Britain's preeminent radiotherapists, in August 1948, she wrote:

Thank you very much indeed for your generosity in sending me a complimentary copy [The Treatment of Malignant Disease by Radium and X-rays]. It is a pleasant and instructive reminder of my months in Manchester and I have told you before, they were quite the most rewarding of the many I spent in post-graduate work.

Dr Trapp maintained a close friendship with Ralston Paterson and his wife Edith, as witnessed by the extensive correspondence between them on various matters including grateful thanks from Edith on receipt of a care package of fruit sent by Ethlyn shortly after the war. Several years after the war she continued to send care packages to friends in Germany and England established before the outset of war.

In a letter from The White House, Congleton Road, Alderley Edge, Cheshire in January 1952, Edith Paterson wrote:

My Dear Ethlyn, I should have written immediately to thank you for the most welcome and generous gift of butter. What could be more welcome yet I know that even if it is easily obtainable in Canada it remains a most expensive present, so I must put in a chiding for the extravagance of it all!

In January 1955 Ethlyn wrote to Ralston Paterson at the Christie Hospital in Manchester: *"Dear R. P. It was nice to have Edith's note on your Christmas card bringing me up to date with the family interests."*

When Dr Simeon Cantril of the Swedish Hospital Tumor Institute in Seattle came to Vancouver in 1948 to consult on a patient at the request of Dr Trapp she wrote: *"I am sorry that Mary Grace cannot come with you for the weekend. My spare room is at your disposal and I suspect that I could make you more comfortable than in the hotel."*

Writing to Dr Walton in Winnipeg in response to his coming to Vancouver in the summer of 1955 she wrote: *"If you are coming complete with children and camping equipment as you suggested you might, I should be only too glad to have you pitch your tents in my garden."*

Her friendship with Ralston Paterson is further evident in their correspondence prior to his visiting the BCCI in 1957 at the request of the British Columbia Cancer Foundation *"to review the Foundations organization of therapy services."*

Paterson wrote on February 4, 1957:

I have had a very warm and cordial invitation from J. H. Lamprey The President of your British Columbia Cancer Foundation, to visit. The reasons are:

a) Participant in post-graduate course to the Medical profession.

b) Survey of the Foundation's organization of therapy services.

I wonder if you could let me know purely informally and unofficially

1) Are you behind this invitation or is it spontaneous?

2) Can you give me any ideas as to what the real task would be?

Trapp responded on February 9:

Your letter of February 4th arrived yesterday and I am going to find it difficult to answer. Too much background—problems building up over a period of years—anyway I will begin with your questions.

1) I am not behind the invitation in the sense you mean. The idea that somebody from the outside could be a help in smoothing out a difficult situation and so improving the services of the Institute really came from organized medicine, specifically the Board of Directors of the British Columbia Medical Association. When it was put to Max [Dr Maxwell Evans] by his Board of Directors he asked to have you—a suggestion which I naturally supported as did the other medical members of the Board. At the same meeting it was suggested that a Canadian Doctor might be asked to accompany you—somebody familiar with the Canadian scene such as Harold Warwick or Clifford Ash.

2) The real task is I think improving public relations—i.e. with the rest of the Medical Profession. The number of patients admitted to the Institute has been falling off, and this disturbs the Board of Directors as well as the Provincial Department of Health which underwrites 80 to 90% of the running expenses of the Institute.

In a follow-up letter on May 3 she wrote:

I have procrastinated about this letter because I hardly know what to say. The difficulties at the Institute have been building up over some years and came to a climax when Dr Moffat [a senior radiotherapist in the Institute] resigned stating he had been prevented from doing his job in a conscientious fashion. There were other complaints and a clash of personalities. Following this, Mr. Lamprey, the President of the Foundation met with the Board of Directors of the B.C. Medical Association and there were subsequent meetings with his own Board. The outcome of all this was Mr. Lamprey's letter to you.

I, myself, am in no position to give an opinion about the radiation therapy at the Institute because I have had no connection with it since 1945 when I resigned to give the job back to Max on his return from Overseas. Since then my association has been as a member of the Board of Directors and of the Honorary Attending Medical Staff so that I am only at the Institute to attend their respective meetings. Perhaps this will explain why it is difficult for me to help you."

After spending five days at the Institute, Dr Paterson attended the BC Cancer Foundation Board and his remarks were reported as follows: "*he felt privileged to visit with the members of the Foundation and to observe the work done here. He congratulated the members on the magnificent Institute which they had established and of which they could be very proud.* He went on to offer suggestions "*made in no spirit of criticism but rather as an analysis of the work of the Foundation that they were setting out to accomplish.*"

Ethlyn and Emily Carr

Ethlyn Trapp became a close friend of Nan Cheney in the late 1930s. The friendship probably arose through Trapp's association with the radiologist Dr Hill H. Cheney on his move to Vancouver General Hospital in 1937.

Anna Lawson Cheney (1897–1985), born in Windsor, Ontario, was an aspiring artist in Ottawa when she married Dr Cheney in 1924. Anna (Nan) Cheney met Emily Carr in Ottawa in 1927 and again in 1930 on a summer visit to her aunt Mary Lawson in Vancouver. Carr always referred to her as "Nan." Following their move to Vancouver in 1937, Cheney and her husband bought property beside the Capilano River in West Vancouver in 1940.[41] Nan Cheney became a well-known BC portrait painter and the first University of British Columbia medical artist. She met and corresponded with many Canadian artists and formed a strong friendship with Emily Carr.

Nan Cheney's correspondence with Emily Carr and Humphrey Toms reveals Emily Carr's association and friendship with Ethlyn Trapp. In her later years Nan became a close friend of Nell Lawson, a niece of Dr Trapp and daughter of T. D. Trapp, eldest of Thomas Trapp's children.

Emily Carr, a prolific painter, suffered failing health in the late 1930s and turned to the writing of both books and correspondence with others, particularly Nan Cheney. These letters present the first indication of her meeting with Dr Trapp.

Cheney must have mentioned Trapp to Carr, for in a letter dated January 25, 1938, from Carr to Cheney, Carr had written: *"Will be pleased to meet Dr Ethelyn (sic) Trapp"*[42] and on February 16, 1938, she wrote, *"I did enjoy you & Dr Trapp what a nice person."*[43]

Carr's writing in her letters was as colourful as her paintings, full of spelling and grammatical peculiarities, but fascinating to read. Most of her writing was done in the last few years of her life when she was an invalid and often confined to the house. She ended one letter to Nan Cheney: *"Now for decencies sake (just to set an example to the unemployed) I must arise. & tub. Wow! It's dark & raw. There's a great deal to be said for hibernation."*[44]

Dr Trapp undertook a speaking engagement in Victoria on Friday, November 25, 1938. We may wonder how she travelled to Victoria. Did she take a car or travel as a foot passenger? We can surmise that she may have taken a CPR Princess liner. The Canadian Pacific Railway Company's Princess fleet had for more than half a century provided the means for people and goods to move from Vancouver to Nanaimo and Victoria. The Union Steamship Company provided similar links to coastal communities northwards along the British Columbian coast. The Pacific Princesses were smaller versions of the Empress liners that crossed the pacific to the Orient. Though smaller, the Princess ships provided similar comforts and opulence as their larger sisters. Two of the fleet's finest ships were the *Princess Kathleen* and the *Princess Marguerite* that plied the "Triangle Route" between Vancouver, Victoria and Seattle, as well as the overnight Vancouver to Victoria run. These and others of the fleet also made daytime runs from Vancouver to Victoria and travelled between midnight and 7.00am, which might have been preferable to some. The *Marguerite* sailed from Vancouver at 10.30 AM arriving in Victoria at 3.10 PM and left at 4.30 PM to arrive in Vancouver at 9.00 PM. The *Kathleen* and the *Marguerite* carried primarily foot passengers, each licensed to carry 1500 passengers, but provision was also made to allow transport of 30 automobiles.[45]

If Dr Trapp had crossed on the *Princess Marguerite*, she might have shared some of the opulence experienced by King George VI and Queen Elizabeth on their visit to Canada in 1939, when they sailed from Vancouver to Victoria at the end of their cross-country rail journey. Dr Trapp would have embarked in Vancouver at Pier B-C—Pier D, the normal berth of the Princess liners, having been destroyed by fire in July 1938, four months before Dr Trapp's speaking engagement in Victoria.

On the Vancouver to Victoria route, the car would have been carried on the main freight deck. On the larger steamers, cars were loaded through doors on the sides of the vessels and then manoeuvred into parking spaces in rather tight quarters. Some of the ships like the *Joan* and *Elizabeth* had turntables for cars to make it easier to get them on and off. Dr Trapp also visited Victoria twice in 1940. Again she may have sailed on the *Kathleen* or the *Marguerite*, because it was not until 1941 that the two ships were withdrawn from the Triangle Route and sent to Europe for wartime service.

When Dr Trapp visited Victoria in July 1940 "on business," she again planned to meet Emily Carr. That "business" may well have been to check on 100mgm of radium that had been loaned to St Joseph's Hospital by the BC Cancer Institute twelve months previously. Dr Trapp, who was acting Medical Superintendent of the Institute in Vancouver in place of Dr Evans who had left for military service overseas, had been told by Sister Mary Alfreda RN, of St Joseph's Hospital in Victoria, that Dr K. Bibby was in charge of the radium. Perhaps Dr Trapp was not altogether sure of Dr Bibby, so in September she contacted Dr Frederick O'Brien of Boston, Massachusetts, who confirmed that Dr Bibby was indeed qualified to use radium.[46]

After the visit, Emily wrote to Nan Cheney: "It was such a pleasure & surprise to see Dr Trapp. I enjoyed her visit greatly & hearing about you from an eyewitness."[47]

Dr Trapp's concern for the plight during the war years of friends she had made in training in Europe in the 1930s surfaces in a letter from Carr to Nan Cheney: "*Poor Dr Trapp what a consignment!*" (Trapp had agreed to look after the wife and three young sons of Dr Bannerman of Edinburgh as evacuees during the war. She had spent some time in the last year of her undergraduate medical training in Edinburgh in 1927) *"It is hard on people. I do think evacuees should be allowed to bring some contributing sustinence. For my part I think I'd s[t]ay among the boms. Maybe when one fell on my hat, I'd up & scoot."* [48]

Trapp asked Nan Cheney to use Emily Carr's technique to do three portrait sketches of her nephews and niece at $7.50 each. Nan commented in a letter to Humphrey Tom *"hardly worth doing—however I would do a lot for her."*[49] At the time Cheney was not well and it seems unlikely that she did the sketches.

Dr Trapp visited Emily again in November 1940. Emily recorded the visit in a letter to Nan Cheney dated November 18, 1940: *"Thank you ever so for the crabs. They look delicious have not sampled yet. but am shure we shall enjoy them. It was good of Dr Trap[p] to tote them, and I am glad she had the excuse or she might not have found time to give me the delightful visit which I did so enjoy. I know she has many friends & plenty to do when she comes over she is a dear soul."* Later in the same letter she described how Dr Trapp took with her to Vancouver *"Macdonald's picture."* (This was Carr's oil painting "Cabin in Woods," which the 1940 graduating class of Templeton Junior High School was presenting to the school.) *"It was good of her & such a help these odd canvass[es] are such a nuisance to post. too small to crate but must be protected or express refuses exceptance. well thanks for the pickles I'll eat your helth in them."*[50]

This painting was placed on permanent loan to the Vancouver Art Gallery.

For many years the painting lay in the vaults of the Gallery until brought to the fore for the benefit of this publication. The picture is reproduced in black and white, though the original is in the dramatic browns, greens, blues and greys typical of Emily Carr's well-known paintings.

Emily must have sent Ethlyn a copy of her first book *Klee Wyck*, because Ethlyn wrote to thank her from San Francisco, on Fairmont Hotel notepaper, in November 1941:

My dear Emily Carr—It seems I must get away from home to find time to tell you how delighted I am with "Klee Wyck"—it comes up to all expectations which is saying a good deal—my first copy I have sent off to a friend in Australia—it isn't often that one can make such a happy choice of Xmas gifts.

Had a delightful evening at the McGeers just before I left when Ira read some more of his "Emily Carr Note Book." It is a never failing source of pleasure to us all—my aunt, Miss Dockrill, was also there and heard them for the first time & was most enthusiastic.

I'm here for a few days to attend a medical meeting—San Francisco is a lovely place, my room overlooks the Bay and at this moment it is like fairyland in spite of the discordant notes of the traffic. We often speak of your visit to Vancouver and hope you will be repeating it in the

Fig 28. Macdonald's picture. Acquired by the Templeton Secondary School Grade 9 class of 1940. Emily Carr, Cabin in the Woods, oil on canvas, 55.9 x 40.6 cm. (Collection of Vancouver School District #39; Photo: Tim Bonham)

spring time when the weather is more propitious, for one of our travels "Crescent" is still asking for you to come there. Affectionately yours Ethlyn Trapp."

"Crescent" would be the property on Christopherson Road near Crescent Beach. It is not known when Ethlyn acquired the property that stood on a bluff overlooking Boundary Bay, just south of Crescent Beach, with a railway line below the cliffs close to the beach. It seems likely that this would have been after her parents' deaths in the early 1930s. Perhaps the property at Sunnyside across from Port Moody moved more to the Dockrill family that had first settled there.

Crescent Beach had become much more accessible when the new Great Northern Sea Line route opened in 1909 from Vancouver to Brownsville via the Fraser River Rail Bridge, west along the south bank of the river and across flat lands to Mud Bay, Crescent Beach and White Rock. At that time the main rail traffic between Vancouver and Blaine was diverted from the New Westminster Southern Line.

Fig 29. The Trapp property near Crescent Beach photographed in the late 1940s. A family Buick is in front of the house. (Photograph courtesy of Lynn Roseman)

By 1918 White Rock was the most important of Surrey's three ports of entry from the United States. With the coming of the railway, people were able to detrain at Crescent Station and then hike the two miles to Ocean Park. Initially the Great Northern Railway authorities had refused requests for a station at Ocean Park. However, in 1912 campers built a small shed station at the foot of the hill beside the tracks and GNR accepted it and agreed to stop one train a day each way on flag. By the time Ethlyn and her sister Neita owned the property, there were morning and evening runs with stops at Crescent Beach, Ocean Park and White Rock and people from Vancouver and New Westminster had an opportunity for weekend or summerlong vacations at the beach.[51]

When Emily Carr visited the property and planted an acorn there in the spring of 1942, she may have travelled by train to Crescent Beach or possibly Ethlyn drove her from Vancouver. This may have been the only time Emily visited because later in the year her health had deteriorated.

Ethlyn and Neita each transferred their interests in the three plots to their nephew Dr W. G. Trapp who then deeded one plot each to his three daughters. The property is no longer in the family.

Fig 30. The oak tree that grew from an acorn planted by Emily Carr stands to this day lopped of lower limbs to confine its six decades of growth. (Photograph by the author)

Emily Carr replied to Dr Trapp's November letter in December 1941, the letter being hand delivered by Ira Dilworth, Emily's trusted friend who acted as editor and devoted supporter of her writings.[52]

By October 1942, Carr's health was failing and she was now in the Mayfair Nursing Home in Richardson Street, Victoria. Dr Trapp visited her on three consecutive days. Carr wrote to Ira Dilworth:

"Wasn't she liberal in her short time? She had on lipstick!! Didn't know she wore it—but I love her all the same, though it did not go with her severe mannish hat." It was during these visits that Emily first told Dr Trapp that she wanted her to have one of her "sketches" and that she should go and choose one. Trapp had said. *"I might if it was some people's choice but I would be quite content with Ira's."* Dr Trapp had taken glorious red roses from her garden but did not tell Emily much about her new house on the banks of the Capilano River. Emily later told Dilworth in a letter describing Dr Trapp's visit that she wanted him to tell her all about the house.[53]

Writing to Emily in November 1942, Ira Dilworth mentioned that he had met Dr Trapp during lunch that day and that at the recent Red Cross sale, one of Emily's pictures had brought the highest price of almost $55.[54]

Perhaps in response to Emily's request to Ira Dilworth to hear more about the new house, Dr Trapp wrote from Vancouver on November 20, 1942:

My dear Emily Carr,

How nice of you to write to me & how I should love to have a pre-view of "The Pie" so I hope that Ira may sometime have a spare hour in the midst of his terribly busy days. (This letter from Emily to Ethlyn is not available to the author; however, "The Pie" refers to a manuscript on which Ira Dilworth was working.) *Capilano is lovely these days & daily with the falling leaves the mountains come more clearly into view & the city lights are twinkling in the distance by the time I get home from the office. You must come and see it for yourself. In the meantime you might think of a suitable Indian name for the place—its former name was "Riverside.". I only hope that you may fool your doctors once again & with your extraordinary vitality—who knows? & even if your body is to remain inactive your spirit may have all the greater scope. After all you did not begin your sketches in writing until you were flat on your back. I have had "The Book of Small" for some days—it is delightful—such fun to read again the familiar ones and to have the new. The whole family are loving it & it will be so useful for Xmas presents for the elect. The Red Cross auction is going very well—yours had the highest bids the last time. I'm just off to have dinner with Nan—she is very nervous these days—it's too bad she couldn't be like the Virgin Mary with her inner quietness.*

With much love
Yours ever Ethlyn Trapp

On December 12, 1942, Ethlyn sent a telegram of congratulations to Emily for her birthday the following day.

Carr wrote to Trapp in May 1943 whilst she was away from Vancouver and the letter was forwarded to Ethlyn in Chicago. Ethlyn replied from the Drake Hotel, on Lake Shore Drive, on May 31:

My dear Emily Carr—Your letter was forwarded to me here to-day & I felt really touched that you should use up your precious strength in writing to me—I had no idea that you had taken the asthma as well. It is really too bad. I know how very distressing it can be. How you have the energy to put on a one man show I can't imagine—an inner compulsion I suppose that transcends physical considerations. I'm thankful I shall be home in time to see it—at the moment I'm doing a bit of a busman's holiday—was becoming dissatisfied with my work so thought I'd best do something about it. Chicago is a city with a tremendous roar & on hot days like to-day I wonder why I left my lovely peaceful Capilano—like minds compulsions! It's nice to think of you at home again—hospitals no matter how good are just hospitals & become very wearying & I like to visualize you with your dogs & birds at hand & in your accustomed surroundings. [Carr was always surrounded by dogs and birds and in earlier times even had a pet monkey]

In the same letter, Trapp wrote further:

I have a snap or two of our bit of the Capilano which I brought to show my sister in St. Paul & will enclose these, hoping that they may entice you over when you are stronger & Emily dear I hope you will be feeling much better & happier when this reaches you—when you are discouraged think of what you have accomplished in one life time & what you will be leaving to posterity—a really valuable Canadian heritage. Most of us are not so privileged— it is people like you who are beginning to make us realize that we really are a nation & have a country to be proud of. With very much love, Ethlyn T.

& like the Virgin Mary I ponder in my heart."[55]

In a letter to Ada McGeer, Carr wrote:

I told him (Mr Dilworth) *that I would like to give away about six sketches to people who I thought would really like to have them. Yours, Dr Trapp's and Walter Gage's were such happy gives and gave me great pleasure. I don't feel these things are entirely ours to keep, any more than music is, but should be shared with those who enjoy them. They are not given us just to keep.*[56]

Dr Trapp took home two of Emily's pictures with the intention of choosing one. In October 1943 she wrote to thank Emily:

My dear Emily Carr,

I can't begin to tell you what a thrill your picture has given me & continues to give me every time I walk into my living room. I collected it the night before last & Nan & Hill came down with two screw hooks & the necessary & we hung it immediately, first above the fireplace, where it definitely didn't belong & then on the long wall, where it dominates the whole room & where I can look at it from my favourite seat—Thank-you so much Emily dear for your generosity. It will be a source of pleasure for many besides myself. I have already thanked Mr Dilworth for making such a happy choice—the other I liked too but feel it was not quite so inspired. Also I must tell you what pleasure my brief visits with you last week gave me—it was an inspiration for me as a medical woman to see how far the spirit can dominate the flesh & I shall be looking forward to two bites of the "Pie" when I shall again visualize you as you talked with me about it & other matters. Please hurry & get well enough to come to Vancouver again. I know you will love our spot on the Capilano & I must take you to Crescent again. In the meantime I shall hear of you often from Ira [Dilworth]—what a good friend he is & what a good friend he has in you.

With much love & again thank you, affectionately,
Ethlyn Trapp

The picture that Ethlyn chose, the first of several of Emily's that she came to own, was an early Carr watercolour of a young girl holding a fan. The picture was painted in 1909 and titled *Seated Young Girl*. Carr painted at least one other portrait of a seated girl in 1909 and it is housed in the Vancouver Art Gallery.

In 1906 Emily Carr had moved from Victoria to Vancouver and opened a studio on Granville Street to give art classes to children. The studio was a wonderful place for children, with cages filled with squirrels, chipmunks, raccoons and bullfinches, a parrot and a cockatoo. Billie the sheepdog and white rats were allowed to run free. The older children sat at easels and copied Miss Carr's plaster casts of a hand, a foot or a horse's head. If they remained and progressed, they advanced to watercolour and finally to draw from a posed model.[57] It was surely one of those models that was also the young girl that Emily painted and which, later, Ethlyn chose as a gift.

As Ethlyn acquired more Carr paintings in her later, more stylized depiction of trees and forests and native artefacts, the serene young girl may have seemed out of place and Ethlyn moved it to her entrance hall at Klee Wyck to the right of the front door where it hung above a table and telephone.[58] Dr Trapp loaned the picture she had chosen thirty years earlier to hang in the Emily Carr Retrospective Exhibition of 1971–72 in Vancouver and Toronto.

At the time Ethlyn had received the picture, Carr's pictures were being sold for about $250. Her oil on canvas Quiet, which had been offered by Ira Dilworth for that amount, sold for $1,121,250 in 2004.

In a photograph of Ethlyn in her living room in Klee Wyck, taken about a year before her death, there are three paintings visible on the wall. Ethlyn is seen entertaining a young friend and her daughter to afternoon tea. It is summer and there is a large bowl of freshly picked roses from her garden on the table. There are bread, butter and pound cake on the table to be had with tea from an "Everhot" teapot. On a stroll in the garden later the little child fell into and was duly rescued from one of the inviting duck ponds. The furthest wall in this photo-

Fig 31. Seated young girl with fan. Reproduced in black and white. Emily Carr, *Seated Young Girl*, 1909, watercolour. Photocopy from Doris Shadbolt fonds. (Reproduced by permission of the Rare Books and Special Collections of the University of British Columbia)

graph, which Ethlyn referred to as the long wall, is the most likely original location of the *Seated Young Girl*, moved to the front hall when the later Carr paintings were acquired. On the back wall at the extreme right of the photograph is an oil on canvas of trees painted by Emily Carr in 1939 and named *Juice of Life*. Dr Trapp deeded the painting to the Art Gallery of Greater Victoria in her will. Ethlyn owned at least three more Carr paintings including *The Role of Life*, similar in content to the former, and an untitled landscape and an untitled painting of a cottage in Brittany. The landscape is unlikely to be the other painting on the far wall of her sitting room since Carr's canvases were almost always rectangular in shape and the clouds in the painting are not in the "Carr" mode. The third painting in the photograph may have been an early Gordon Smith, since she owned several of his works, or more probably a watercolour by Nan Cheney.[59]

The young woman in the photograph is a further reminder of Trapp's friendship with George Godwin originating in the Balfour Sanatorium immediately after the Great War. The young lady is his granddaughter whose mother, Monica, had visited with Dr Trapp during the few years in the early 1960s when she lived in Vancouver. Dr Trapp also met with Godwin's son Anthony who was on the point of being sent to live with her during the Second World War. He had become a successful lawyer in Singapore and, on flying home to England, stayed over in Vancouver with his two sons. Dr Trapp took the visitors for a drive on the Sea to Sky highway to Squamish.

Extracts from the letters of Carr and Cheney are taken from *Dear Nan: Letters of Emily Carr, Nan Cheney and Humphrey Toms*, edited by Doreen Walker and published by UBC Press, 1990. The letters included in the book contain thirty-five references to Dr Trapp. In the twenty-three letters from Carr to Cheney or Toms, Carr is ever deferential, referring to Trapp on each occasion as Dr Trapp. In Cheney's earlier correspondence, there is the same formality until Trapp moves closer across the Capilano River and, on three occasions between 1943 and 1945, Cheney refers to her as "Et," indicating a growing familiarity in their friendship.

Emily Carr described a visit from Dr Trapp a month later in a letter to "Old Eye" [Ira Dilworth]:[60]

Dr Trapp was here 3 hours. I put her in with the men clan as visitors calm and sane & healing. I told Dr Trapp she'd stolen my fat. I thought her looking so well & much fatter. She said it was a small hat. She looked very nice and pretty little hat & fur coat & it was lovely having her.

This is the last recorded visit between the two friends, and in correspondence Emily always deferred to Ethlyn as Dr Trapp.

In a letter to Emily Carr the day before she died, Ira Dilworth wrote that he had told Dr Trapp that the University of British Columbia planned to honour Emily with the degree of Doctor of Letters at its May 1945 convocation.[61]

Emily Carr died in St Mary's Priory in Victoria on March 2, 1945.

Fig 32. The living room at Klee Wyck in the early 1970s. Photograph taken about a year before Ethlyn's death. (Courtesy of Lucy Godwin)

Klee Wyck

In the spring of 1942, Dr Trapp purchased the property at the end of Keith Road on the west bank of the Capilano River for $8,500; she later deeded the property to the Municipality of West Vancouver. Only five days after her letter to Emily from Chicago, on May 31, 1943, Ethlyn must have suddenly thought of a new name for her house, previously called "Riverside," and wrote to Carr:

"It's only a day or two since I wrote—but an inspiration has come to me & I wonder what you will think of it. You must be entirely frank & if you don't like the idea say so without hesitation. It is this: I'd like to call my house on the Capilano after your "Klee Wyck"—it seems to me entirely appropriate for such a happy place. Think about it & let me know when I return which will be in another two weeks— slightly less—in the meantime I trust that your too active heart is giving you a little peace & that you are feeling a lot better than when you wrote. In haste but with very much love Emily dear.

Yours ever

Ethlyn T.[62]

In June 1959 Dr Trapp's solicitor wrote to the Municipality of West Vancouver advising them that Dr Trapp would like to give her grounds and her home to the municipality on condition that she be given life occupancy and use of the property. Also she would not have to pay any property taxes on the property for the rest of her life. In the following February a formal agreement was signed, in which the property was given on condition that it be used as a park, nursery garden, playground or other purposes of public recreation.

Dr Trapp specified in the agreement that it was being done to *"perpetuate the memory of her father, the late T. J. Trapp of New Westminster."*

Klee Wyck was the Indian name given to Emily by the First Nations People in Ucluelet, on Vancouver Island, and means "laughing one." Permission to adopt the name was apparently readily given by Ms Carr.

Nan Cheney, who lived across the river from Klee Wyck, described the property in a letter to her longtime friend Humphrey Toms in October:[63]

Dr Trapp moved into her house in Sept. [1942] after being here for 6 weeks. You know it is just down the river below Jock's—on the other side & luckily the Keith road bridge is open so we can walk over often. She has quite an estate—with a caretakers house at the gate and a driveway curving round to the house. Several ponds fed from a mountain stream & 5 wild ducks who seem to have come to stay. I redesigned the house for her & if I do say it, the result is well planned & spacious.

Cheney also mentioned that Dr Trapp had two Carr sketches in her big living room. By the following summer she reported that *"Dr*

Fig 33. Ethlyn Trapp in the garden of Klee Wyck with two of the children of her nephew, Dr William Trapp, who stands on Ethlyn's left under the garden umbrella in the extreme right of the picture. The children play by one of the duck ponds in the grounds of Klee Wyck that were so popular with visitors and their children. (Photograph courtesy of Nancy Delay)

Trapp's place is simply lovely now & they have 24 wild ducklings on their ponds. They feed them of course & they are so tame they follow you about."

By December of 1943 she wrote to Toms:

We see a good deal of Dr Trapp—her place is a real estate now—she has a man & his wife living in the cottage at the gate & he is an experienced gardener then she has a pensioner living in another little house & he does all the chores so it is being well looked after. The house is lovely—my design—and Et is very pleased with the whole thing.

Ethlyn's parties at Klee Wyck were frequent and extensive in their guest lists and hospitality. Like old-fashioned "salons" reminiscent of the nineteenth century, many of her evening gatherings included influential people from the art, music and intellectual worlds. For many years there was a wonderful Chinese cook in the kitchen, which was dominated by a wood stove. He baked sour cherry pie with a puff pastry crust, often served with hot maple syrup. The cherries were from a tree in the orchard on the property. At Christmas, Ethlyn would serve mince tarts and eggnog.[64]

Paul Trapp, Dr William Trapp's son, has childhood memories of great events at Easter and Christmas. There were numerous Easter eggs hidden throughout the property and huge vats filled with seeds of all kinds were available for endless feeding to the ducks.[65] Ethlyn took special interest in the children of her extended family, giving birthday parties and presents, often in the form of books. Nancy Delay, Ethlyn's great niece, the daughter of Dr William Trapp, recalled that as a teenager, the books given to her by Ethlyn were meant to encourage thought and awareness of her femininity. She well remembered *The Second Sex*, by Simone de Beauvoir, first published in English in 1953. There are few remaining photographs of these parties and the duck ponds that gave the children such enjoyment. The photograph (Fig 33), provided by Nancy and restored, shows Nancy and Paul, her younger brother, as youngsters feeding the ducks with Ethlyn standing between two adults at the far right. The front entrance to Klee Wyck is on the opposite side of the house from the Capilano River.

Betty Lord, 24 years Ethlyn's junior, became friends with Drs Trapp and Sadler when she worked in the Laboratory of the Georgia Medical Building. She recalled the many outings she had with the two doctors, though "she never had their kind of money," as well as the numerous cocktail parties at Klee Wyck with the rich and famous coming and going. She shared the same favourite drink as Ethlyn, scotch and soda. Betty and Olive Sadler owned a boat and a cottage on Thetis Island.[66]

When Dr Trapp retired from practice in 1960 she decided "*after a year of domesticity and all that it involves life must hold more than keeping oneself alive.*" The outcome was that she returned to university, this time at UBC as an undergraduate in horticulture. There was of course an underlying motive for this decision in that she had a large garden and plans for an improved commercial venture. Ethlyn had started three years previously with the aid of a good Swiss gardener, but after a succession of mediocre gardeners, she gave up the project. Perhaps in an effort to keep the good gardener supervising her land, she planned to change her will in 1955 and wrote to her solicitor:

I wish to add a new paragraph which concerns my gardener, Roger Fotsch and his family. If he so wishes, I should like him to remain in the cottage at the gate and continue to have charge of the garden. To facilitate this my estate shall pay him the sum of $150.00 a month for six months and in addition let him keep one half of the net earnings from the greenhouse.

Despite this generous offer, perhaps gardener Fotsch and his family were homesick and so returned to their homeland in the beautiful city of Solothurn. Ethlyn and her great niece Nancy visited the Fotsch's on their tour through Europe, on route to the 8th International Cancer Conference in Moscow in July 1962. Solothurn, situated at the southern foot of the Jura mountain range, is described as Switzerland's most beautiful baroque city and the city of culture. Ethlyn often took a companion with her on these trips for company and to share the driving. On this occasion, as they drove from Munich through Switzerland and Austria to Paris and Moscow, Ethlyn was quite happy to let her eighteen-year-old inexperienced companion, Nancy Trapp, do most of the driving. Ethlyn also had a poor sense of direction, another reason for taking a companion or family member with her, which was often her physician nephew, Dr William Trapp.

Ethlyn's first year at UBC was followed by courses taken in the department of anthropology and sociology. Throughout her life she read widely in psychology, religion, politics, art and music. She had shown a lifelong interest in the BCMA's Library and on her death bequeathed money to the Library to purchase books of medical history and biography. As a strong supporter of the World Health Organization she had arranged a subscription for *World Health* to be placed in the Library. Each Christmas she arrived a day or two before the holiday with a special hand-picked box of confections for the staff.[67]

Dr Trapp's return to university opened new worlds for her and, over her remaining years, she became involved in the World Federalists of Canada and the United Nations Association in Canada. Of course her interest and involvement in her garden and animals remained firm, as a member of the Royal Horticultural Society and the West Vancouver SPCA.

Not long before her death she travelled to the Skagit Valley to take part in a rally opposing its flooding. (The Canadian portion of the beautiful Skagit Valley was saved from flooding in the late 1970s by the British Columbia Government compensating Washington State for the loss of power that they would have been able to generate through damning the valley).

Dr Trapp quite often gave lectures to nurses. Her association with the Federation of Medical Women of Canada resulted in the establishment of the Ethlyn Trapp Memorial Scholarship in Medicine. These scholarships are still offered to UBC students in second-, third- or fourth-year Medicine, with preference given to students with demonstrated interest in women's health.

Her love for travel continued and in 1971, at the age of 80, she accompanied her lifelong friend Ada McGeer to the Galapagos Islands.

Dr Trapp had many friends and was close to her sister Neita Collishaw, who lived in West Vancouver on Ottawa Avenue, and to Nan Cheney, who lived across from her on the Capilano River. Following the war, Raymond Collishaw had joined his family in West Vancouver at 2627 Ottawa Avenue, a home they owned for over 50 years. There

Fig 34. Photograph of Raymond and Neita taken in the garden of their home in West Vancouver in the fall of 1945. (Raymond Collishaw and R. G. Dodds, Air Command: A Fighter Pilot's Story [London: William Kimber 1973])

were two plots but later a new house was built on the one adjacent to the original house that still stands overlooking English Bay and from which Vancouver Island can be seen in the distance.

Back in civilian life, after nearly fifty years in uniform, Collishaw was kept busy in various mining enterprises. His first venture was a placer mining operation in the Barkerville area of British Columbia. Hydraulic equipment and high-pressure hoses that washed the gold-bearing gravel into sluice boxes worked well, but the operation had to be closed down because of the deflated price of gold at the time. Outstanding amongst various mineral exploration and development enterprises in the next two decades was Craigmont Mines, of which he was president for five years. The shares rose from 10¢ to $21.50 during his tenure and the company's copper mine became the largest in Canada.

Collishaw died peacefully on September 29, 1976, at the age of 82. He was buried with full military honours after a simple service at St Stephen's Anglican Church. The flag-draped casket bearing the Air Vice-Marshall's military cap was carried by hand up 23rd Street to the Upper-Levels Highway and transported to the Capilano View Cemetery. A "Fly-Past" of four voodoo jets and notes of the "Last Post" ended a short graveside service. His wife Neita was buried with him thirteen years later.

Money Matters

In her letters Ethlyn mentions an unnamed companion with whom she had spent many summers, and who she had hoped would live with her in retirement but who had died prematurely. (In her will she named the friend as Margaret B. Pickel and left $10,000 to Columbia University in New York to establish a scholarship fund "to keep the memory of so worthy a friend.") These summer trips had involved explorations into the interior of the province "mostly camping, surface cots and sleeping under the stars."

In 1962 Ethlyn offered Klee Wyck for rent from April to October for $350 per month, though her letters do not record whether or not this venture was successful.

There are many references to Ethlyn being careful with money yet, at the same time, always generous. When she was wrongly credited with money from airplane tickets on one of her many trips it took more than a year for her to accept that she had actually received the money and so returned it. She had to be reminded to pay a bill of $12.00 for the digging of a trench and laying of a water pipe on her property on Christopherson Road at Boundary Bay. This was her property on a shoreside road separated from Boundary Bay by a railway line.

After a visit to Montreal in February 1957, she sent the following letter to Madame Riche:

Your parcel arrived in excellent condition soon after my return home. It is a pity that I was unable to remain in Montreal for another fitting for both the dress and the skirt need a little adjustment. The dress I can have fixed here but I am wondering if I should return the skirt for your expert attention especially as it seems to me that the overlapping part of the wraparound would be better lined. The broadcloth is so thin that it is inclined to wrinkle and to stick to the underlying skirt. It was nice to see you and your staff again and thank you for looking after my commissions so quickly. Looking forward to hearing from you. P.S. I should be glad to have the pieces of the remaining material in due course. E.T.

As the letter suggests, Ethlyn was a careful and attentive dresser. She had a special closet built in Klee Wyck with foldout sections for her many dresses. She was particularly fond of browns, tans, sage green and beige, and paisley silk scarves.

Olive Sadler referred to Dr Trapp's "private fortune." How did she accumulate the wealth to travel all over the world, to spend years in postgraduate training, much of it in Europe, and to purchase expensive equipment for her office practice and several acres on the Capilano River in West Vancouver? In her twenties she worked in a military hospital in Vancouver and in a sanatorium as an occupational therapist, which would not have contributed to any fortune. In her thirties she travelled to the Far East and the Antipodes and returned to McGill to study medicine. No money was earned there. In her forties she tried general practice, assisted a radiologist at St Paul's Hospital and spent half the decade in travel. No riches can be found there. In her fifties and sixties she was part-time medical director of the BC Cancer Institute and in private practice. In the specialty of radiotherapy at that time it is hard to imagine anybody becoming wealthy. So where did her "private fortune" come from? Her father became wealthy through investment in property and land and may have avoided the losses at the time of the great depression. Did he arrange for substantial monies to be transferred to his children before, or perhaps soon after, the Great War? We shall never know, though it is clear that Ethlyn must indeed have had access to substantial funds to support her travels. The $8,500 she paid for Klee Wyck and the grounds on the Capilano River seems a real bargain by today's West Vancouver standards, but at the time was a considerable sum. The subsequent arrangement with the municipality of West Vancouver to avoid property taxes for life was a shrewd move demonstrating an astute awareness of financial matters. At the time of her death her estate was valued at close to $200,000.[68]

It seems likely that Ethlyn invested in her brother-in-law's mining ventures when he returned from England at the end of the war. However, that was long after she had purchased Klee Wyck and close to her retirement. Some of Collishaw's ventures were not successful. In May 1962 Raymond Collishaw wrote to Ethlyn about the Copper

Mountain Mines Ltd at Deep Gulch telling her that the shareholders were asked at the annual meeting to take a cutback of 5 to 1 in all the issued stock of the company. In the letter, he likened it to an amputation. Collishaw himself lost 500,000 shares. It is not clear how much Ethlyn lost, but one might guess that she would have been much more cautious.

In one of her last letters, approaching the final two years of her life, she expressed her sadness at the present: *"no peace anywhere, desperate labour troubles etc. etc. and so much of it all based on pure greed"*. She reflected on her West Vancouver property:

My own particular spot on the Capilano remains a peaceful one though drastically changed from when I 1st came here nearly 30 yrs ago. When there was only a foot bridge across the river—now a noisy and light flooded highway. Vancouver itself is a traffic hazard and I go only when I must—Stanley Park relieves the situation to some degree especially when one drives around it rather than through when going or coming—fortunately it has been jealously guarded by the city fathers and kept relatively free for the enjoyment of young and old.

Following Ethlyn's death in 1972, Ada McGeer recalled *"the many nights when after dinner"* she would leave at the end of a gathering at Klee Wyck, and her hostess *"would stroll along with me to my car and we would stand savouring the fragrance of the garden. Enclosed by the tall firs on one side and the rushing river on the other, the duck ponds reflecting the stars above us."*

George

Ethlyn's devotion to medicine, her eagerness for travel and further education, her ability to make friends around the world, her fondness for gardening and her boundless generosity are among the measures of a full and satisfying life. But was she loved, did she love? What was it that made her write that her life was *"not as I would have chosen"*?

What happened to her in the postwar years in the early 1920s before her decision to become a doctor and return to McGill is not recorded. However, some of that time can be surmised from George's letters, written to her in 1939–1941 and again in 1970. The letters are housed in her personal correspondence file, given to the Vancouver City Archives by a friend on her death. The letters give a taste of forbidden fruit and unrequited love, hidden from others, even her friends and family, for nearly half a century. Although not a great beauty, throughout her professional life she engendered strong feelings of affection in male colleagues and, indeed, their wives and families. She was friendly, thoughtful, warmhearted and generous, and must have carried a certain feminine allure. In a letter of congratulation following her delivery of the Osler Lecture in Vancouver a male colleague wrote of *"the charm and femininity"* of the speaker.

From the time they shared together in Balfour at the close of the Great War and the later letters of George Godwin, it is possible to piece together some of Ethlyn's early adult life, and perhaps find a reason for her to pursue medicine, devote her life to cancer care and perhaps also to remain single and childless.

The following paragraphs are taken from Godwin's letters, though many of the inferences are the author's and may not necessarily be accurate.

In the first letter, dated October 17, 1939, George is replying to a letter from Ethlyn, perhaps written after the pair met while Ethlyn was travelling in Europe prior to the opening of the British Columbia Cancer Institute. It is written from 43 Curzon Street, W 1 London, on the letterhead of the Acorn Press. The letter is handwritten and six pages long. He writes at length about his five children, their successes and failings. Then perhaps in response to a recent meeting he wrote:

I knew instinctively that when we lunched that day we were out of rapport. Ah, my dear, life is surely "a tale told by an idiot". Please remember that I shall always welcome the sight of your handwriting and all that you do, dear Ethlyn, interests me still. Though I've been long silent I often think of you.

The letter ends: "*I kiss you as of old, George.*"

Mention of a lack of rapport may suggest that the "love" was somewhat one sided. The letters of Ethlyn to George are not available, but those from George continued to be effusive.

Now that first letter is pretty strong stuff. What have the years hidden? We have to go to his last letter in May 1970 to begin to understand the background. The letter was written when George was 81, two years before Ethlyn's death and four years before his own:

Fig 35. George Godwin.
(Courtesy of Godwin Books, Victoria BC)

From the enclosed few snaps I had at hand you will have revived for you some memories of those far-off days in the San when I first found that I loved you. I shall write you again, dear Ethlyn, and I hope you will write again to me. So I embrace you in memory.

As ever George.

So what is the reference to "San"? It was of course the Balfour Rocky Mountain Military Sanatorium on Kootenay Lake, in British Columbia, which operated from 1917–1920, after which the building was demolished in 1928. It was there, shortly after the First World War, that an occupational therapist helped a war veteran with tuberculosis towards recovery. The patient was the writer of the letter, George Stanley Godwin.

Godwin, born in 1889, developed into a rebellious schoolboy in England and, at the age of fifteen, was sent to Germany with his eldest sister who was studying singing. When his mother died in 1911 he came to British Columbia and sent for his fiancée, Dorothy Purdon, the daughter of a Belfast physician. The couple married and for four years, from 1912—1916, cleared land at Whonnock on the Fraser River. In those four years, a son, the first of five children was born. The homesteaders failed miserably, returning to England in the summer of 1916. He joined the Canadian infantry, fought in the trenches at Vimy, developed tuberculosis, was invalided back to England and sent to the Balfour Sanatorium in British Columbia's interior for one year. After the year, with his illness arrested, George returned to England and heard that, at the time of Passchendaele when he lay invalided in England, he had been called to the bar. He never returned to Canada.

George became a prolific author whose work included twenty-one books. His four years in Canada and his war experiences produced two acclaimed books. These were *The Eternal Forest*, in which a central character called the "Newcomer" vividly portrays pioneer life in the Fraser Valley, and *Why Stay We Here?* a philosophical and critical response to the war. The books never received the recognition they deserved and fell out of print. The two mentioned have been reissued by Godwin Books in Victoria in the last few years.

Ethlyn was a keen traveller throughout her adult life. When

attending scientific meetings, she would always take a day or two, if she could, to get to know people and the area. In her postgraduate studies she spent time in all the major cancer centres in Europe. In her early twenties the urge to travel took her to many parts of the world, reaching as far as New Zealand. It was there that she made the sudden decision to become a doctor, returning to Canada to enrol in medical school at McGill. How much of this travel and the sudden decision to enter medical school were the actions of a young woman who had been shown the love of a married man, a forbidden fruit that the daughter of a pillar of the Presbyterian faith could not enjoy? We do know that she never married and had no further contact with George until the late 1930s.

In a second letter dated December 1939, now that they were back in touch, George is rather petulant: *"Just one*

Fig 36. Ethlyn Trapp at the "San." Image reproduced from a 3X4 inch snapshot that Godwin sent to Ethlyn with the single word "You" written on the back. (Ethlyn Trapp, Personal Correspondence, City of Vancouver Archives, 513-F-1, File 4)

grumble. Why did you keep away from me while you were so long in England [Manchester e.g.] That was naughty of you." (Trapp had spent six months in 1937 as a Resident Medical Officer at the Christie Hospital and Holt Radium Institute in Manchester and had also been to London to meet with Dr Constance Wood.)

By the summer of 1940 the war was becoming a serious affair in England. The opportunities for writing had dried up and George had to sell his house and move to two rented rooms in Harcourt Buildings, Temple, EC 4 London. In response to a gift from Ethlyn, who recognized his change in circumstances, he wrote:

Ethlyn, I'm going to take the tenner you enclosed and accept it as a loan until I am round this confounded corner. Thank you very much for a real pal's act I shant forget it, for it is when one is all raw inside that such actions mean so very, very much.

Lots of love, dear Ethlyn,

From your George.

In the letter he described how the government had plans to evacuate children to Canada to escape the bombing of London and raised the possibility of his youngest son, Tony, being part of the scheme and living with Ethlyn. Of course, she immediately promised to take him in and George responded:

I hope with all my heart that this can be brought off, for then, whatever befalls the rest of us, at least something of the seed will be planted upon good soil. I could ask for nothing better for any boy of mine than to come within the orbit of your spiritual influence and I told Dorothy of that. Once more thank you a thousand times. Personally, I would so gladly return to Vancouver, but it is not to be. Meanwhile, all my grateful thanks to you for this extended hand in times of great difficulty.

Your very affectionate, George.

Early in 1940 the British Government had initiated schemes to evacuate children from London and other major cities under bombardment, to live in the countryside where there would be less danger from German bombs. They also encouraged the sending of children to Canada or Australia. By the summer, over 1,000 children had arrived safely in Canada. Godwin and his wife had felt that their youngest, Tony, should be offered the opportunity to escape the risks and they were both thrilled that Ethlyn had offered to take the boy. The scheme was made available for children of grant-aided schools such as Perse School in Cambridge where Tony was a pupil, making him eligible for transport. Forms were completed and he was medically examined and passed. But then there were doubts officially. The scheme was suspended for a while, then reinstated, but finally abandoned for good with the ghastly sinking of one of the ships. The *City of Benares* was torpedoed on September 17 at dead of night in fierce seas 600 miles into the Atlantic crossing. There were 406 people aboard, 90 of whom were children, and only 13 of the little ones survived. The *City of Benares* had been built as a luxury liner on the Clyde in 1936 and was named after the holy city on the Ganges. Prime Minister Churchill ordered a stop to the evacuation of British children to Canada on September 23, two days before the last of the survivors were rescued.

As conditions in London worsened, George wrote from the Temple in August 1940:

Maybe, too, you get hectic stories of the air raids, so let me tell you that here, again, we are perfectly well and thank-you-very-much. It is now perfectly understood that Jerry will try with increasing vigour to smash down our morale, but had you been in London these last few days when we have had warnings and bombs in the suburbs, you would know how stupid are those Germans who imagine that this sort of thing, even in progressively larger doses is going to put the wind up the people of England. I am so glad you remembered the Temple lawn and I am glad to be able to tell you that it stands as it did when you last saw it, green and smooth and bathed in deep peace.

My love to you, George.

You may ask, when did Ethlyn see the Temple lawn so green? This is difficult to determine, for in one letter George refers to a luncheon meeting in which they did not get on too well and another where he complains that she had not got in touch with him while she was in Manchester in 1937. There is no record of Ethlyn travelling to London in 1938 or 1939; indeed, she was involved in her private practice and the establishment of the BC Cancer Institute as a member of a three-person committee charged with supervising the use of irradiation facilities by the BC Cancer Foundation. In 1935 and 1936 she had been in Europe visiting centres in Brussels, Berlin, Frankfurt, Paris and Stockholm, so was it possible that she stopped for a visit when passing through London to meet with Constance Wood at the Radium Institute? If so, did she not tell George that she was going to spend several months in Manchester? Dr Trapp's files do not reveal more and information concerning Godwin at that time does not exist.

In December 1940 Ethlyn sent George a Christmas parcel, and he replied:

Of all the nice things I found in your welcome gift I think my eyes popped most at those two tins of butter. About Tony. We entered him [in the evacuation scheme] and gave notice at school. Then there was that ghastly tragedy when the Unspeakable swine sank a ship load of kiddies 600 miles at sea without warning (Im through with Germans for ever).

With the cancellation of the evacuation scheme, Tony never did come to Vancouver to live with Dr Trapp. Despite bombs and land mines severely damaging the Temple, George ended the letter in an optimistic note: "*The terrors of air warfare on London, like the accounts of Mark Twain's death, are grossly exaggerated. WE CAN TAKE IT.*"

Despite his bravado, on the night of New Year's Eve, a few short days later, George was severely injured when a land mine demolished the next-door house and he was thrown through a glass door, requiring "*14 stitches and two operations, but I am no Clarke Gable now.*" Within hours of his rooms being damaged, they were looted:

They took three things: my gold watch, the cash in a little tin box and THE TEA YOU SENT ME! I was almost as wild about the tea as about the watch. All the best to you, my dear and consider yourself kissed by England's ugliest man. As ever, George.

The letters from George die away in 1941 and are only resumed nearly thirty years later in 1970. Although Ethlyn must have responded, not only with gifts but in word, none of this correspondence is available to us. There are, however, handwritten notes, highly edited and altered which appear to be made in preparation for two letters to George in

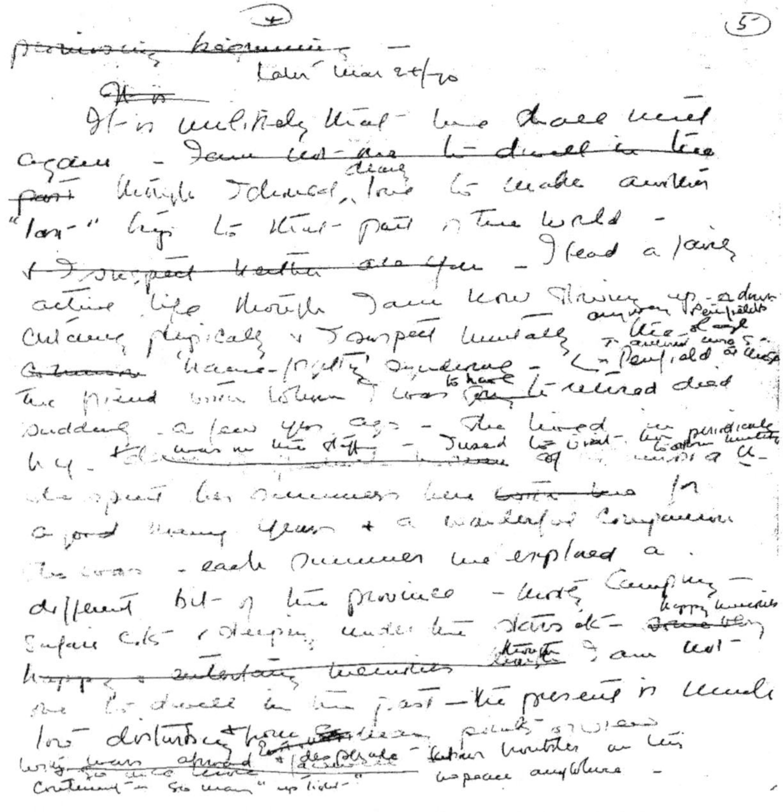
(4) (5)

~~promising beginning~~ —

Later Mar 24/70

~~It is~~

It is unlikely that we shall meet again — ~~I am not one to dwell in the~~ ~~past~~ though I do not dwell, love to make another "long" trip to that part of the world — I lead a fairly ~~& I suspect neither do you~~ active life though I am now slowing up — a down curve physically & I suspect mentally [illegible] 'name-forgetting' syndrome — [illegible] The friend with whom I was to have retired died suddenly a few yrs ago — she lived [illegible] I used to visit [illegible] spent her summers here ~~with me~~ for a good many years & a wonderful companion she was — each summer we explored a different bit of the province — [illegible] camping — [illegible] sleeping under the stars etc — [illegible] I am not [illegible] to dwell in the past — the present is much too disturbing [illegible]

Fig 37. One page of notes for Ethlyn Trapp's last letter to George Godwin.
(Ethlyn Trapp, Personal Correspondence, City of Vancouver Archives, 513-F-1, File 4)

1970. We know they were sent because George refers to them in one of his last letters from England.

In the notes, dated March 20, 1970, she refers to the memoirs that George had sent of his son Geoffrey, who had drowned during a second crossing of the Atlantic in 1968, and a 1939 letter from George that *"came to light a few months ago as I was cleaning a desk drawer. I cannot begin to tell you how pleased I am that you decided to send the memoir to me. I read it through with hardly a pause & a deeply emotional experience it was learning so much of you and your family & a dip into my own past."*

Later she refers to how they are both getting old:

It is unlikely that we shall meet again though I would dearly love to make another "last" trip to that part of the world. I lead a fairly active life though I am now slowing up, certainly physically & I suspect mentally—the "name-forgetting" syndrome. I am not one to dwell on the past—the present is much too disturbing from many points of view—wars—desperate labour troubles—etc etc—& so much of it all based on greed—no wonder the young rebel."

She further laments: "Like you I am now old—my life has been a fortunate one in so many ways— though not as I would have chosen."

Ethlyn Trapp died on July 31, 1972, at the age of 81.

Appendix

Origins of the Trapp Name

The name "Trapp" came to British Columbia with Thomas and Samuel, brothers who left their native Essex in 1872 for Ontario and Victoria the following year.

The Trapp name, sometimes spelled with a last letter "e," was a common name in England. The name came from the occupation of hunters, or "trappers." The word "Traeppe" was the Old English word for snare.

British History on line reports that Carreg Cennen castle, on a hilltop overlooking the Welsh village of Trapp, was taken by the English in 1278. Joseph Trapp is mentioned as rector of Cherrington Church in Gloucestershire from 1662–98. He was probably the father of John Trapp who was curate from 1698 and rector from 1700.

Perhaps the most famous Trapp was John the Divine (1601–1669, sometimes given as 1611–1669). An Anglican with Presbyterian sympathies, John Trapp wrote a large and very popular commentary on the Bible. The work is famous for its pithy, quotable style and its sayings were frequently reported. In writing on the claim that a person might have a hand in his own salvation (arminianism), Trapp the Puritan wrote, "*The friends of free will are the enemies of free grace.*" He taught at William Shakespeare's old School in Stratford upon Avon. John Trapp came to the School in 1629. During the Civil War he sided with the Parliamentarians, becoming chaplain of the Stratford garrison. Following the recapture of the town by the Royalists he was taken to Oxford and imprisoned there for a time.

The name Trapp has become common in the United States, especially in the Eastern States. There are two theories as to the origin of the English Trapp name in the United States. Both are based on Martha's Vineyard and revolve around a Thomas Trapp. One account has a Thomas Trapp sailing on a ship from England to Virginia in the early 1630s. For a variety of reasons, Trapp and three other families requested to be put ashore near present Edgartown. Here they became the first settlers of Martha's Vineyard. The second account, which is historically supported, is that Thomas Trapp arrived at the Vineyard in 1659 on the ship *Exchange*. He was about 25 years of age. While it is possible that the 1659 Thomas is the son of the first, this has not been confirmed. The Thomas Trapp that arrived in 1659 quickly became entrenched in the Vineyard's affairs. Besides acquiring land holdings on the island, he served as a marshal, water bailiff and crier in 1667, a juryman in 1679, a deputy sheriff from 1694 to 1700 and town clerk from 1700 until his death. He married a woman named Mary around 1674, and they had nine children: John, Samuel, Simon, Ann, Thomas, Mary, Jabez, Mercy and Hannah. Thomas died in 1719, and is buried in Tower Hill Cemetery in Edgartown, on Martha's Vineyard.

This branch of the family eventually spread to Connecticut, New York, and later to the Midwest States and California. One branch has been traced to New Zealand. Many southern United States families have the same name. Varieties of the name have been found to be "Trapp" or "Trappe."

Another branch, also from Essex, part of the so-called Brownists evaded the persecution in England between 1604 and 1608, by going to the Netherlands. Later, part of that group became well known as the Pilgrim Fathers.

Possibly the earliest known of the Trapp family that later came to Canada is John Trapp who in 1762 was reportedly the first Waltham Abbey member of parliament from Woodward in Essex. Over one hundred years later, Thomas John Trapp, son of Thomas Trapp, a forest ranger for Sir Heribwald Wake, and surveyor for the town of Waltham Abbey in Essex, emigrated to Canada in 1872. We do not know Ethlyn's grandfather Thomas's date of birth but he died at the age of 66. In some records he is listed as married to Elizabeth Guy. However, the Trapp family gravestone in the Fraser View Cemetery in New Westminster includes an inscription for Eliza Pollard, Wife of Thomas Trapp, Eliza having died at the age of 79 in 1893. This may be the same Eliza Pollard who was baptized on August 6, 1815, in Tingewick in Buckinghamshire. We can assume that after the death of Thomas, his widow Eliza came to live in New Westminster with her son and his family. Were Eliza and Elizabeth the same person with some confusion over the name Guy or had Thomas been married twice? We shall never know, but we do know that the gravestone clearly refers to Eliza Pollard as the wife who followed Thomas's sons to New Westminster.

Notes

(1) M. A. Cleaves, "Radium; with Preliminary Note on Radium Rays in the Treatment of Cancer," *New York Medical Record* 64 (1903): 601–606.

(2) Juan del Regato, Radiological Oncologists: *The Unfolding of a Medical Specialty* (Reston, VA: Radiology Centennial, 1993), 234.

(3) Robert Reid, "Pierre Curie and Autobiographical Notes by *Marie Curie*," in Marie Curie (New York: Saturday Review Press, 1974).

(4) Thomas J. Trapp, *The Trapp Motors Story*, Special Collections, Port Moody Library.

(5) "Gretchen Schafer's 1871 Diary, Travel on the Transcontinental Railroad," Central Pacific Railroad Photographic History Museum, www.cprr.org/Museum/index.html.

(6) Robert D. Turner, *The Pacific Princesses* (Victoria: Sono Nis Press, 1977), 7.

(7) Roger Boshier, "Manipulative Technologies, 1873," www.edst.educ.ubc.ca/tern/Chrono/ManThen.htm

(8) Turner, *Pacific Princesses*, 4.

(9) The Native Brotherhood, "Culture Contact in Southern Alaska," Senate Doc. 59, 34, 1879, www.alaskool.org/projects/nativegov/documents/anb/anb-2.htm.

(10) Alan Macek, "Walter Moberly," The Early Years of the CPR in BC, www.alanmacek.com/canyon/people/Moberly.

(11) Greenwich Mean Time.com, "The History of Time Zones," www.greenwichmeantime.com/info/time-zones-history.htm.

(12) British Columbia.com, "Tete Jaune Cache," www.britishcolumbia.com/regions/towns/?townID=3991.

(13) John Tait, "The Murder of John T. Ushher," History Articles, Kamloops Archives, www.city.kamloops.bc.ca/museum/archives/archive-index.html.

(14) "T. J. Trapp Makes Good in the Wild West," *Lougheed Mall Discover*, Spring 1991, 35.

(15) Trapp, *Trapp Motors Story*.

(16) D. M. Norton, *Early History of Port Moody* (Surrey: Hancock House, 1987).

(17) City of New Westminster, "History of New Westminster Fire & Rescue Services," www.city.new-westminster.bc.ca/cityhall/fire/history.htm

(18) Jack Brown, "Surrey's History: Brownsville," City of Surrey: A History, members.shaw.ca/j.a.brown/Surrey.html.

(19) Brown, "Surrey's History: Early Settlement Centers," members.shaw.ca/j.a.brown/EarlyCenters.html

(20) J. A. McPhee, "Building with a Macabre Past," *The British Columbian*, May 21,1955, 1-4.

(21) G. Basque, "Legend of the Lost Creek Mine," in *Lost Bonanzas of Western Canada* (Langley, BC: Sunfire Publications, 1988).

(22) McPhee, "Building with a Macabre Past," 1-4.

(23) Lara Kozak, "The Rise and Fall of All Hallows School in Yale, BC," The Gold Rush Town of Yale: All Hallows, www.bcheritage.ca/yale/tour/hallows.htm

(24) Jean Barman, "Indian and White Girls at All Hallows School," in *Indian Education in Canada*, Vol 1, edited by J. Barman, Y. Hebert, and D. McCaskill (Vancouver: UBC Press, 1986).

(25) Hour.ca-News-Babylon, PQ, Jamie O'Meara, "Will You Stay or Will You Go?" Babylon Archives, PQ, www.hour.ca/redirect.aspx?iIDReaction=9713

(26) Raymond Collishaw and R. G. Dodds, *Air Command: A Fighter Pilot's Story.* (London: William Kimber, 1973).

(27) George Godwin, *Why Stay We Here?* (Victoria: Godwin Books, 1994).

(28) British Columbia Cancer Institute, Brochure to commemorate the opening of the new building (1952), BC Cancer Agency Archives.

(29) BC Cancer Foundation, Minutes, 12 June 1935, BC Cancer Agency Archives, Box 7, UI 200.

(30) BC Cancer Foundation, Annual Report, 1970: Report of the Director, BC Cancer Agency Archives.

(31) BC Cancer Foundation, Campaign Committee, *British Empire Cancer Campaign 1933—1947*, BC Cancer Agency Archives, Box 40, UI 1198, File #1.

(32) BC Medical Association, Committee on the Study of Cancer, Minutes, BC Medical Association Archives.

(33) BC Cancer Foundation, Board of Directors, Minutes, 20 June 1941, BC Cancer Agency Archives, Box 24, UI 992.

(34) BC Medical Association, Correspondence, 1938-1943, BC Cancer Agency Archives, Box 19, UI 928.

(35) BC Cancer Institute, Honorary Attending Staff, Minutes, 11 May 1942, BC Cancer Agency Archives, Box 3, UI 101.

(36) BC Cancer Foundation, Board of Directors, Minutes, 13 April 1943, BC Cancer Agency Archives, Box 24, UI 992.

(37) BC Cancer Foundation, Board of Directors, *Statement to the Minister of Health*, 10 July 1944, Correspondence, BC Cancer Agency Archives, Box 24, UI 992.

(38) Ethlyn Trapp, Personal Correspondence, City of Vancouver Archives, 513-F-1, File 2.

(39) Ibid., File 4.

(40) "Olive Sadler: An Appreciation," *British Columbia Medical Journal* 4(8) (1972): 1219.

(41) Doreen Walker, ed., *Dear Nan: Letters of Emily Carr, Nan Cheney and Humphrey Toms* (Vancouver: UBC Press, 1990), xliv.

(42) Ibid., Letter 29.

(43) Ibid., Letter 30.

(44) Ibid., Letter 135.

(45) Robert D. Turner, personal communication, 2005.

(46) Stewart Jackson, *Radiation as a Cure for Cancer: The History of Radiation Treatment in British Columbia*. (Vancouver: BC Cancer Agency, 2002), 35.

(47) Walker, *Dear Nan*.

(48) Ibid., Letter 162.

(49) Ibid., Letter 172.

(50) Ibid., Letter 173

(51) Brown, "*The Great Northern Sea Line Route*," members.shaw.ca/j.a.brown/Surrey.html

(52) Linda M. Morra , ed., *Corresponding Influence: Selected Letters of Emily Carr and Ira Dilworth* (Toronto and Buffalo: University of Toronto Press, 2006), 65.

(53) Ibid., 154, 160.

(54) Ibid., 175.

(55) Ethlyn Trapp, Letters, BC Provincial Archives, Add MSS 2763, Box 4, File 61; and the BCMA Archives.

(56) Ada McGeer in *Oh Call Back Yesterday, Bid Time Return* (Vancouver: Versatile, 1981).

(57) Maria Tippett, *Emily Carr: A Biography* (Toronto: Oxford University Press, 1979).

(58) Nancy Dilay and Betty Lord, personal communications, 2005.

(59) Walker, *Dear Nan*, Letter 237.

(60) Morra, *Corresponding Influence*, 251.

(61) Ibid., 298.

(62) Ethlyn Trapp, Letters, British Columbia Archives and Records Service, Parnall Collection, MS-2763, Box 4, File 61.

(63) Walker, *Dear Nan*, Letter 231.

(64) Nancy Dilay, personal communication, 2005.

(65) Paul Trapp, personal communication, 2005.

(66) Betty Lord, personal communication, 2005.

(67) "A Further Bequest," *British Columbia Medical Journal* 16(10) (1974): 10.

(68) Lynn Roseman, personal communication, 2009.

Select Bibliography and Suggested Further Reading.

Barman, Jean, Y. Hebert, and D. McCaskill, eds. *Indian Education in Canada*. Vol 1. Vancouver: UBC Press, 1986.

Basque, Garnet. "Legend of the Lost Creek Mine." In *Lost Bonanzas of Western Canada*. Langley, BC: Sunfire Publications, 1988.

Carr, Emily. *Klee Wyck*. With foreword by Ira Dilworth. Toronto: Clarke, Irwin, 1965.

Carr, Emily. *The Emily Carr Omnibus*. Introduction by Doris Shadbolt. Vancouver: Douglas & McIntyre; Seattle: University of Washington Press, 1993.

Collishaw, Raymond, and R. G. Dodds. *Air Command: A Fighter Pilot's Story*. London: William Kimber, 1973.

Curie, Eve. *Madame Curie, a biography by Eve Curie*. Garden City N.Y.: Doubleday, Doran and Co, 1937.

Godwin, George. *Why Stay We Here?* Victoria: Godwin Books, 1994.

Godwin, George. *The Eternal Forrest*. Victoria: Godwin Books, 1994.

Howay, F. W. and E. O. S. Scholefield. *British Columbia Historical*. Vol 3. Vancouver: S. J. Clarke Publishing, 1914.

Jackson, Stewart. *Radiation as a Cure for Cancer: The History of Radiation Treatment in British Columbia*. Vancouver: BC Cancer Agency, 2002.

Jackson, Stewart. From Dough to DNA: *601 West Tenth, Vancouver—the Bakers, the Building and the BC Cancer Research Centre*. Vancouver: BC Cancer Foundation, 2004.

Morra, Linda M., ed. *Corresponding Influence: Selected Letters of Emily Carr and Ira Dilworth*. Toronto and Buffalo: University of Toronto Press, 2006.

Norton, D. M. *Early History of Port Moody*. Surrey, BC: Hancock House Publishers, 1987.

Turner, Robert D. *The Pacific Princesses*. Victoria: Sono Nis Press, 1977.

Tippett, Maria. *Emily Carr: A Biography*. Toronto: Oxford University Press, 1979.

Trapp, T. J. *The Trapp Motors Story*. Nd. Port Moody Library Special Collections.

Walker, Doreen, ed., *Dear Nan: Letters of Emily Carr, Nan Cheney and Humphrey Toms*. Vancouver: UBC Press, 1990.